BEAR CHARM

SHIFTERS BEWITCHED #2

TASHA BLACK

13TH STORY PRESS

Copyright © 2021 by 13th Story Press

All rights reserved. This book or any portion thereof may not be reproduced or used in any manner whatsoever without the express written permission of the publisher except for the use of brief quotations in a book review.

13th Story Press
PO Box 506
Swarthmore, PA 19081
13thStoryPress@gmail.com

Cover by Natasha Snow of Natasha Snow Designs.

TASHA BLACK STARTER LIBRARY

Packed with steamy shifters, mischievous magic, billionaire superheroes, and plenty of HEAT, the Tasha Black Starter Library is the perfect way to dive into Tasha's unique brand of Romance with Bite!

Get your FREE books now at tashablack.com!

BEAR CHARM

1

CORI

Mine.

The word echoed through my head as I awoke alone in my bed.

I was trembling and heated, my cheeks flushed. The remnants of the dream were evaporating too quickly, leaving behind only the memory of a muscular male body pressed to mine, and the echo of a deep roar.

No.

That last bit wasn't fading at all.

That raw, animal growl was real. It split the air again, along with a dull pounding from somewhere far above.

My eyes went automatically to Bella's bed, but my friend and roommate was gone now. I was on my own.

I sat up, listening hard. Maybe the dream really was just bleeding over into reality.

The castle was silent, the air strangely cold and coppery.

I closed my eyes and tried to recall the dream, but all I could remember was a pair of glowing, golden eyes, and the feel of strong arms pulling me close.

Those eyes, they reminded me of something, of someone...

There was another roar, the notes of anguish clear, even in such a primal state.

I slipped out of bed without thinking and headed into the hallway, inexplicably drawn to that sound.

My regulation nightgown flowed out behind me. Primrose Academy loved tradition. Witches in training had been wearing these billowy white nightgowns since the school was founded. Truthfully, I kind of liked it.

Once I got out into the hallway, it was clear that the sound was coming from the tower.

I reached the stout wooden door that led to the tower stairs, and paused for a moment to think. Students weren't allowed to go up to the tower, everyone knew it. And just in case anyone forgot, a sign had appeared on the door a few days ago, reminding us of that fact.

The tower is off limits to students at all times.
- Headmistress W. Hart

Another moaning sound echoed from above.

My heart pounded, but I needed to know what it was. The sound felt like it was reverberating in sympathy with my own heart, and I had to find the source. I tried opening the door, but it wouldn't budge.

There was only one thing to do.

Cori, no...

But I didn't have a choice. Something was pulling me up into that dark tower, and I wasn't about to stop until I found out what it was.

I squeezed my eyes shut and called on my power, even as I cringed at the thought of the outcome.

Things usually went wrong where my magic was involved. My friends said magic as powerful as mine was always unwieldy in the beginning. But they were just being nice, like friends are.

I knew the problem was me. I was too timid, too nice to really take control of my gift. That weakness in me sabotaged my magic every time.

At least I would need so little of it this time that it could hardly go wrong. And had been preparing as much as I could, so hopefully I wouldn't have to pay much of a price for it.

The price of my magic was high, when I really used it. Too high to waste it on anything that wasn't super important.

I cupped my palms and concentrated.

There was the usual tingling sensation in my hands as my magic rose to the surface, lifting its senses to take in the light.

I pushed and pulled, shaping it into what I wanted. My magic was elemental and finicky, and it stretched like taffy before finally succumbing to my will.

At last, I felt moisture in my hands and opened my eyes.

A tiny thunderstorm hovered over my open palms. The puffy gray cloud roiled and rumbled like the purr of a cat, releasing a mist of rain.

The first time I'd managed this. I had been so charmed by the storm that I tried to cuddle the little thing.

But I learned the hard way that even a palmful of lightning had a nasty bite. Hopefully, just enough to open a door.

"Okay, Misty, do your thing," I murmured to it, holding it against the lock just above the handle.

Purple lightning flashed. The first tiny bolt headed right for me, but I managed to dodge it. I was pretty sure the little storm hated my nickname for it.

"You little rascal," I scolded.

The second lightning strike hit the door right in the keyhole. A resounding click told me the lock was released. Thin smoke rose from the site.

"Good work," I told the impudent little storm.

It rained down even harder on my hands so that water dripped through my fingers onto the floor.

"Okay, okay," I told it. I was sapped anyway, there was no point holding onto it. "You can go."

I closed my eyes and released the magic.

The tingling sensation was gone. The only traces left behind were the small puddle and the light scent of ozone.

My hand closed around the doorknob and then things went hazy.

What am I doing here?

It seemed to be the middle of the night, but I was in the hallway, in my stupid nightgown.

There was a sign on the door I was trying to open.

The tower is off limits to students at all times.
  - Headmistress W. Hart

I was going to the *tower*?

My hand dropped away from the doorknob like it was burning.

Students weren't allowed up in the tower, everyone knew it.

My heart pounded and I ran my hand through my hair. I

must have been sleepwalking, or... I shook my head to clear it, trying desperately to remember.

The price of my magic was confusion, and short-term memory loss. So I was used to having to piece things together anytime I unexpectedly used magic.

Had I been using magic? For what?

If I had come here in the middle of the night and used magic without paying for it in advance, I must be in some kind of trouble. No witch would casually pay the price for magic when her price was as high as mine was.

There was a groan from somewhere above and then a thud.

Everything came back to me in a heartbeat. I sighed in relief. I had succeeded in unlocking the door to the tower.

I was still doing something stupid, but at least I remembered deciding to do it. I twisted the knob before I could change my mind, and began climbing the stairs.

I don't know what I expected. It's not like I thought there would be a fancy elevator or anything. But I hadn't pictured the endless circle of stairs winding up and up and up.

I gathered up my gown in my hands and moved as quickly as I could, pulled like a magnet to whatever was at the top.

At intervals I would pass a window showing me the darkened grounds of the school. As I got higher, the view shifted to one of the nearby treetops under a blanket of stars.

Here on the mountaintop, the stars were visible every night. It was nothing like the bustling suburban hub where I'd spent my childhood.

I could almost believe I was a real princess in a castle from medieval times, stealing away in the night. Except that storybook princesses were always tall and graceful with long, pale hair.

And I was short and curvy with a mop of dark, unkept curls and no innate grace or charisma to speak of.

If this were a fairy tale, I would be the luckless scullery maid, trotting up the tower stairs to bring the kindling for the princess's fire, noticed only if I were eaten by a dragon or if the princess did me a kindness.

There was another groan from above and I redoubled my efforts, my panting echoing back to me on the cold stone walls.

At last, legs burning, I reached the top of the stairs. There was another door, just as sturdy as the one at the bottom.

Moonlight poured in a window at the landing, revealing strange etchings on the door.

No, they weren't etchings. They were claw marks.

I lifted my hand to trace them in wonder. They were furrowed deep into the hard wood. Whatever made them must have been huge.

Suddenly something on the other side of the door rasped in a deep, panting breath.

I pulled my hand back quickly, forgetting that I had been tracing the claw marks. A splinter lodged itself in the pad of my index finger and I cried out.

The sound echoed around me as I ripped the splinter out. A drop of blood welled up in its place.

I was putting my finger to my mouth when the thing in the tower slammed itself into the door with a thunderous crash. I half expected the door to splinter to shreds and whatever it was to explode out.

I screamed and flew down the stairs, nightgown flying out behind me.

The steps were endless, and the darkness seemed to close in all around me. My heart pounded so loudly in my ears that I couldn't even hear whether or not I was being pursued.

At last, I burst out of the lower door and back into the main corridor, crashing headlong into something.

"Ow, hey," a familiar voice said angrily.

"Kendall," I said in relief, patting her arm and then reaching behind myself to be sure the door to the tower was locked.

It was.

"Damn, Cori," Kendall whispered. "Watch where you're going."

"I'm so sorry," I told her, grabbing her arm. "But there's something up in the tower."

"Shh," she said, snatching her arm back. "We can't get caught in the halls after midnight."

I watched in shock as Kendall hurried away to her room.

She was fully dressed, I realized belatedly, and wearing make-up.

Of course I had heard the rumors that Kendall had a townie boyfriend, but I hadn't really believed them. The witches of Primrose Academy were supposed to remain celibate as we learned to harness our powers. We were told this was one more way to pay in advance for our magic.

Well, most of us were, anyway.

Of course, there was also the school's arrangement with the guardian shifters who patrolled the forest to help us protect the sacred library.

Every month, under the light of the full moon, we held a ceremony in which a shifter could choose a mate from among the students. Only the guardian shifters never showed up. At least, not in the time I'd been at the school.

Until Bella.

She'd been chosen last month, on her very first day at the school.

I felt a pang of sadness about losing Bella to the guardians. I would miss having her as a roommate. At least she was still coming to school during the day, so I hadn't lost her as a friend. And I knew she really loved Luke, the guardian who chose her.

Bella had her mate, Kendall apparently had her boyfriend in town. Who else was sneaking off for some action? Was I the only witch in the castle who wasn't getting that kind of attention?

Of course, some fumbling townie boy probably wasn't really worth the effort. A guardian, on the other hand…

The golden gaze from my dream came back to me and I gasped.

I did know those eyes. They belonged to the guardian who had come back to the school with Bella and her mate. The one who had stared at me until I flushed and looked away, overwhelmed by his masculine beauty.

I scurried back into my room and crawled into bed, expecting to feel afraid. I was alone, and there was something in the tower, something big. I had heard it, and practically felt it.

And it had noticed me. It had scented my blood.

But as I thought back to the gashes in the door and the anguished roar of the thing in the tower, somehow, I didn't feel scared.

I felt exhilarated.

2

CORI

The cafeteria was bustling the next morning, like it was just another normal day. The scent of maple syrup and coffee filled the air along with the soft chatter and clinking silverware of my fellow students.

I grabbed my breakfast and stood at the end of the line, looking around.

Bella was with her mate, of course, so she usually didn't show up for breakfast. And Anya had a special lesson before class this morning. Nina and Lark were nowhere to be seen. I suspected they had eaten early and headed to the library. They had both worked hard to translate the page that had been ripped from the book Bella had "borrowed" from the library. And now they were trying to track down the sources of all the components for the spell outlined on the page.

The original page was in the hands of the Order of the Broken Blade now, after a run in with a nasty warlock that I'd rather not think about. Fortunately, Nina's note-taking spell had provided us with a copy of our own. And once we figured out the most likely locations of the rare spell ingredients, Bella could relay them to Luke, and the Brotherhood of Guardians could do their best to keep them out of the hands of the warlocks.

The last thing we needed was a group of fanatics trying to bring back the Raven King for their own dark purposes. Anya didn't think such a thing was even possible, and I was inclined to agree. But just the fact that the Order was working so hard to make it happen was reason enough to try to stop them.

Which meant that everyone had been busy lately, and today, it meant that I had to sit with Kendall and her friends for breakfast. I stifled a sigh.

Kendall was a little snobby and a lot aggressive, but she was part of our Bellwether house, and seemed to like me, even though she pushed me around sometimes.

She was easy to deal with on her own, but when she was around her legacy friends, she could be a downright bully. I didn't like the effect Esme and Dozie had on someone I called my friend.

I briefly considered taking my breakfast outside instead of joining her.

"Cori," Kendall yelled to me, ruining my thoughts of a private breakfast on the lawn. "Come here and tell these guys what you told me last night."

"What do you mean?" I asked stupidly.

"That thing you said about the tower," she said, grabbing my tray and placing it on the table in front of the seat next to hers.

I surrendered and sat down. "It was nothing," I said, looking down at my toast.

"Did you really see the ghost?" Esme asked, placing her own toast down primly and leaning forward with interest.

"What ghost?" I asked, unable to resist.

"Actually, there are *two* ghosts," Dozie said in a bored

way. Though in fairness, Dozie said almost everything in a bored way.

"Don't mess with me," I said, rolling my eyes and taking a bite of buttered rye. For being so far off the beaten path, Primrose Academy sure did have some fresh bread. I wondered idly if there was some kind of magic involved. There seemed to be some kind of magic involved in just about everything here.

"We're not kidding, Cori," Esme said. "We would never kid about the ghosts."

"It wasn't a ghost," I said, taking a sip of coffee and grimacing at the bitterness. Whatever magic they were using to keep the bread fresh, it must have been all used up by the time they got around to the coffee.

"What exactly did you see?" Kendall asked.

"There are claw marks on the door," I told her. "Other than that, I didn't actually *see* anything. But I heard roars. And when I got up there, something flung itself against the door. Something big."

"That's the ghost alright," Esme said, nodding wisely to herself.

"Sounds like the man," Dozie said. "He flings himself against the door to get to his lost love."

"The lost love is the other ghost?" I asked, unable to help myself. The business of flinging himself against the door to get to his love actually seemed accurate. The noises had been filled with just that kind of anguish.

"She was a student, and now she wanders the staircases of the school, looking for him," Esme said, her eyes wide. "But because the tower is off limits to students, she never finds him."

My face must have given away the fact that I was considering this scenario. After all, I was surrounded by witches, and my best friend's boyfriend was practically a werewolf. Was believing in ghosts really that much of a stretch?

"Ha," Kendall barked. "She believed it. You really had her going there, Esme."

"Jesus, Kendall," Dozie said moodily. "You weren't supposed to give it away like that. We could have played with her all year."

Esme giggled and wiped her mouth daintily. "You really are very gullible, Cori," she said.

"That was fun," I said sarcastically. "Well, I've got to get moving. Glad you could entertain yourselves at my expense."

"Get over yourself, Cori," Dozie said. "It was just a joke."

I turned to Kendall, but she didn't meet my eye.

Her shame didn't matter though, if it didn't change her behavior. It was clear that being one of the legacies was more important to her than being a friend to me.

I dumped my uneaten breakfast into the trash and headed to the auditorium for morning meeting.

I was surprised to find Headmistress Hart was there already, pacing the floor. Most mornings she swept in after everyone was seated and shouted out a few words of admonishment or encouragement before leaving the school secretary, Miss Twillbottom to very slowly read off the day's announcements.

More students were filing in now. Anya headed my way, and we sat together in the front row.

"Why is she so freaked out?" Anya whispered without even saying hello.

"No idea," I said. "But I'm guessing it's not good."

By now the auditorium was full. Thankfully, Anya had put her books in the seat next to hers to reserve it, so there was still a seat when Bella dashed in just as the lights were dimming. She spotted us right away and moved to join us.

"Women of Primrose Academy," Headmistress Hart said in her loud, clear voice. "As you may have noticed, there have been some changes in our agreement with the guardians."

I could feel all the eyes on Bella. But she sat tall and proud, unembarrassed to be bonded to a guardian and back at school. I smiled, trying to memorize her happy confidence so I could learn to emulate it.

"From now on," Headmistress Hart continued, "any witch chosen for the honor of the mating may choose to continue attending school if that is her desire."

A murmur went through the gathered witches. And although this should have been fantastic news to all of us, there was still a salacious quality to those whispers.

"Furthermore," the headmistress continued, "there have been some other changes. Because of the recent break-in, there will be a guardian on duty in the tower every night, until we get to the bottom of who broke into the library and why."

She went on, but the world seemed to fade away around me as I took in this news.

There was a guardian in the tower.

I pictured the man with the golden eyes and the huge muscular frame.

Was he the one who had called on me in my dreams, pulled me up to the top of the tower in the night and tried to break down the door between us?

I knew that he was here to guard the library, but was he also here... for me?

3

REED

I lope through the trees, massive paws kicking up the fragrance of pine needles and loamy soil.

But nothing can erase her scent.

The memory of it wafts around me like thoughts of summer during a blizzard, and I am lost. She is sweet and pure. She is deliciously sexy - the more so because she doesn't revel in it the way the other witches do.

Mine, my heart sings. She is mine and I will claim her.

Deep inside, my human protests. He believes no woman could love a bear.

But I know better. This mate is different. She will accept both sides of our nature. She has already done so, even if she doesn't know it yet.

Though my human side might have made eyes at her when they met, it was the bear that called to her, this form that she answered.

I can still taste the flavor of her dream, hear her heartbeat from across the castle.

I still revel in the scent of her as she flew up those stairs to me, *her nightgown billowing out with the sharp note of soap and the softer, sweeter scent of a sleeping woman, craving her mate.*

When she cut her finger on the door, I nearly went mad at the fragrance of her blood, slamming myself into the door, desperate to claim her with my bite.

Thankfully, the door held fast. My human side would never have forgiven me for claiming her without her understanding and consent.

But I had to claim her soon.

I wonder where she is and what she is doing. Whatever it is, it can't be as important as sealing our bond.

My human side cries out from my depths, reminding me that tonight is the ceremony at the full moon. If I waited this long, surely I can wait a few more hours.

I push thoughts of her as far from my mind as I can, and the forest around me fades back into my consciousness.

I'm following the faint trail of something that doesn't belong. It winds loosely around the castle grounds, growing slightly stronger as I follow.

The scent is human, so it could be one of the handful of people who come here to camp each year. But I doubt it. The weather is too cold, and this part of the forest is too thick. And something about the scent is just... wrong.

More likely it is a member of the Order of the Broken Blade, searching for magic on the outskirts of the castle campus.

My lips pull back from my canines in a sneer. The fae had organic magic. The witches earn it with their discipline, or by paying a price. The guardians are shifters by nature.

But the Order can only siphon and steal power from others. There is no honor in it, they are thieves like any other, no more noble than the pickpocket at the train station down in the village, though their elaborate ceremonies pretend at greatness.

A new trail joins the old one and I stop in my tracks.

There is a hoof print, and the scent of sulfur.

Fire...

Panic engulfs me and I freeze in place, heart pounding, as my human swims for the surface, convinces me to rest so he can take over.

4
REED

I straightened up into my human form, took a deep breath, and ran my hand through my hair.

Although I handled the idea of fire better than the bear does, I still didn't handle it well. I realized I was breathing in short gasps and forced myself to slow down.

But the memories tore through my brain anyway, and I let them play out. There was no point trying to forget. They were seared on my heart as indelibly as the scars on my back.

They were why I spent most of my life in my bear form. He lived in the present most of the time. The pain of the memories didn't tear him to pieces the way it did me.

I let the memories wash over me, watching the scene play out in my mind's eye.

IN THE MEMORY, it was nighttime, and I was so small, wearing flannel pajamas, curled up like a cat in my mother's bed. I'd had a nightmare, and she had pulled me into her warmth. Still too frightened to sleep, I clung to her, drinking in the comfort of her scent.

The fire revealed itself first by smell, and then by sound. The acrid odor curled into my nostrils and I tried to wake her up again.

"Let me sleep, or you'll have to go back in your own bed," she moaned, unable to detect the danger.

Even then, my superior senses gave me an edge she didn't have.

I would forever be haunted by this moment, the childish side of me too frightened of being alone to forcefully wake her.

A few minutes later there was a keening sound as the smoke detector in our apartment sensed what I already knew.

By the time we were out of bed, it was too late. The door was hot to the touch, smoky tendrils reaching for us from under the frame.

We didn't have a key for the barred window - that was in a kitchen drawer. But as the flames devoured the curtains, I squeezed my small frame between the bars.

"Jump down to the porch roof," she told me. "Tell the neighbors where I am."

"No, no, no," I moaned, not wanting to leave her, knowing there was too much fire. It was already in the room, already upon us.

The flames licked my pajamas and they ignited, the terrible pain distracting me enough for her to give me a little push.

The rest faded - the fall, the burning of my back, the screams of the neighbors, the sirens...

And then my first shift, brought on by pain and fear in

the back of the ambulance. I screamed for my mother until my screams turned to roars.

The guardians got word somehow. They came for me at the hospital.

I knew by then that my mother was gone.

I didn't care about leaving with strangers. I had no one else.

I PUSHED the memories aside and took a deep breath, focusing my mind on the present, on the trail I was following through the forest. All of that was in the past. The scent of an old fire didn't mean new loss.

It was my duty as a guardian to protect, and that is what I planned to do.

I studied the print, drawing on my considerable skills to learn what I could from it.

The impression was large for a horse, but I wasn't sure what other animal would make those crescent-shaped hoof marks. And that was a bad thing. I was an expert on every animal that called this forest home. If I couldn't identify a track, it meant the creature that made it had no place here.

I picked up a handful of earth from the depression and brought it to my nose. The sulfur scent was real and strong.

I straightened and looked around the forest. I patrolled these woods often enough to notice that it had been dry lately. Fire was more dangerous than usual right now. I didn't like this one bit. I had the castle to protect.

More importantly, I had a mate to protect.

My thoughts went to her and my heart surged, adrenaline pumping through my body.

I had to protect her.

I would not lose her to the flames.

I turned back toward the castle, breaking into a run before I'd taken more than a few steps.

5
CORI

I tried my best to concentrate as Professor Sora spoke, pacing primly up and down the classroom as she did. The elderly professor was physically tiny, and her manner was demure, but rumor had it that she was incredibly powerful.

Normally lecture classes were my favorite - the one place where I wouldn't be asked to use my magic, so there wasn't a chance for me to screw everything up.

But today, my eyes were drawn to the trees outside. I wanted to be out there, drinking in the fresh air and the scent of the pine needles. Which was unusual, since I was typically a pretty indoorsy person.

But the cagey feeling was starting to get familiar. It seemed like no matter where I was lately, I wanted to be somewhere else. Like there was a magnet inside me, pulling me away from whatever I tried to focus on.

"Cori, dear, would you like to answer?" Professor Sora asked, viewing me expectantly over her glasses.

I felt the blood rush to my face. I hadn't been paying attention.

"How about you, Nina?" Professor Sora asked instead, with a slight frown.

Damn.

This was the one class where I never got in trouble. I already had so much make-up work in my practical courses for the exercises I'd failed last week.

It seemed like ever since I got to Primrose Academy, I had been waiting for them to finally break it to me that I didn't belong. No amount of make-up work was going to turn me into a witch. Maybe it was better to stay an amateur, or just give it up altogether and try to live a normal life.

Something deep inside my chest rumbled at the thought. My magic, I supposed. It didn't want to be silenced, but it also didn't want me trying to control it. I often wondered what the point of it was.

Bella glanced over at me and raised an eyebrow, clearly wondering what was wrong.

Was I that obvious? I guess I really did wear my feelings on my sleeve.

I smiled at her to show her that I was okay, and then I forced myself to focus on Professor Sora.

"So what are some ways to stop a spell?" she was asking.

My hand shot up. I knew this one. Maybe I could make up some lost ground.

"Cori," she said with a warm smile.

"You can interrupt a spell during its casting," I said.

"Very good, dear, yes," she said, nodding. "Interrupting a spell is the best way to stop it. How else could we stop a spell if we can't interrupt it? Lark?"

"You could cast its opposite," Lark said.

"Yes, Lark, very nice," Professor Sora said approvingly. "We can use a spell for its opposite, like summoning fire to counter a cold spell, or rain to put out that fire. Very good. Anyone else have another idea?"

"What about a counter spell?" Nuria asked from the back row.

"Ah, Nuria," Professor Sora said with a smile. "Counter spells are much more complicated, and they are exactly what I wanted us to discuss today. Kudos to you, dear, for your answer."

Nuria grinned and threw her long black braid over her shoulder.

"Now, the way a counter spell works, is that you primarily use the same components and follow the same procedure for performing the real spell, but with an important twist," the professor went on. "The best way to explain it is to show it to you. May I have a volunteer?"

My stomach sank. Were we really going to have to do demonstrations in a lecture class?

Fortunately, Justine's hand shot up and Professor Sora beckoned the jaunty girl with the pale complexion and the bright red pixie cut down to the front.

"Now we're each going to prepare a simple repairing spell," Professor Sora said, grabbing a crystal vase from her window sill and wrapping it in a cloth.

We all watched as she smashed it brutally against the desk.

She opened the cloth, revealing the shards and dust, gleaming like diamonds.

"Very good," she said calmly to herself. "Now, dear, you're going to cast the repair spell, but I'll counter it."

I watched as they laid out the ingredients and began murmuring incantations.

There were the usual components of a spell - a circle of

material - in this case salt. There was a crystal to represent the glass and a piece of twine to represent joining.

Justine tied the twine to the crystal and swung it in the outline of the circle as she murmured her words. The bits of glass on the cloth began to tremble and move together, like magnets, slowly reforming into the shape of the vase.

Professor Sora waited until the bottom of the vessel was clearly coming together again before she began her own spell.

She had the same circle of salt, the same crystal and twine.

But instead of swinging it in a smooth circle, she swung it violently back and forth.

The bottom of the vase trembled and then fell to pieces.

No matter how hard both women murmured and swung, the glass lay still on the cloth.

"Very good, Justine," Professor Sora said at last. "You may repair it now."

Within minutes the vase was perfect again. Professor Sora watched proudly as Justine carried it back to the windowsill.

"Very nice, dear," she said fondly. "Now class, why did that work?"

"Because they have equal but opposite energy," Nina blurted out.

"Very scientific, dear, but next time raise your hand," Professor Sora said.

Nina nodded and ducked her head down.

"She's absolutely correct," the tiny professor continued. "The energy in each spell is equal, so they cancel each other out. Just like a positive and negative electrical charge."

Electrical charge...

That was what I'd felt when the golden eyed guardian laid eyes on me the other day. But I didn't think there was any spell that could counter the way he made me feel.

My mind went to him, unbidden, and the classroom faded away once more.

6

CORI

The night air was cool and still as we lined up on the cobblestone courtyard.

I shivered, the wet curls hanging down my back practically freezing in place. It seemed unfair that they made us perform a so-called purification in the showers, knowing full well that we'd be sent out into the night immediately afterward for the ceremony.

I'd been at Primrose Academy through dozens of these full moon offerings. They felt like the stuffy ceremonies at the Episcopal church back home - the words repeated so often they became worn and lost their meaning. Until last month, it had never occurred to me that a guardian might actually show up to claim a mate.

I thought back to Bella's pale, shocked face and the electricity in the air between my friend and her enormous shifter mate as they gazed at each other under the moonlight.

The breeze lifted, carrying the scent of pine needles. My eyes were drawn to the tree line, beyond the boxwood maze that separated the courtyard from the woods. There was a tingling in my blood, and I wished I could disappear into those trees.

I closed my eyes and tried to focus on the call and response chant that Headmistress Hart was leading.

"We gather together here in the sacred circle," she said, her voice ringing out against the stones. "*We perform a sacred duty.*"

"We perform a sacred duty," the students chanted back.

"The library shares her sacred knowledge with us," she continued. "*We protect her.*"

"We protect her," we echoed.

I was starting to feel almost faint, swirls of darkness dancing along edges of my vision.

"The library shares sacred knowledge, the witches give their gifts to protect the library," she called out. "*The guardians protect the castle.*"

"The guardians protect the castle," I repeated with the others.

"The guardians give their strength to protect the castle," she went on. "We entrust our fates to the guardians."

My heart was pounding now.

"We entrust our fates to the guardians," I murmured, wondering what was wrong with me. There was no way that a guardian would show up for the ceremony two moons in a row.

Was there?

A brisk wind swirled in the courtyard suddenly, flapping our gowns against our legs. I gasped and searched the maze and tree line again. But there was no movement there.

As one, our group let out a sigh of collective relief and maybe just a little disappointment after the excitement of last month's ceremony.

Headmistress Hart opened her mouth to dismiss us and

I felt a tightening in my chest. I shouldn't feel this way. I was looking forward to getting out of the cold for a nice midnight snack and my warm bed.

Before the headmistress could say a word, an earth-shattering roar split the air.

The women beside me all flinched. Nuria even let out a little cry.

My feet were planted to the ground like they had magma deep roots.

The huge wooden door back into the castle blasted off its hinges with a shriek of twisted wood and metal, crashing to the ground in a heap of debris.

Unbelievably, a massive bear stepped over the rubble and out into the courtyard. He lifted his snout to taste the air, searching for something.

I gulped down the cold night air. This wasn't a ghost - this was what had really been in the tower. This was the guardian whose rasping breaths I heard from the other side of that door.

He stalked around the circle slowly as my classmates cowered and hid their faces.

But I felt no fear, only a sense of numbed wonder.

Me. He was here for me.

As if reading my thoughts, he caught sight of me and picked up the pace, inadvertently knocking into a stone statue with his hindquarters.

There were screams as it hit the cobblestones and shattered.

But he kept moving until he stood in front of me.

In the back of my mind, I noted that it was the same statue I had already broken once before, and wondered if it could be repaired again. Even mending spells had their limits.

I held perfectly still, waiting at the approach of the beast.

His breath misted in the air and I had never felt so aware in my life. I took in every hair on his shaggy body, every droplet of his breath on the cold air, and the dizzying warmth of those golden eyes.

He extended a massive paw toward me, his movement slow, but frightening nonetheless. The size of that paw, of those claws... he could kill me without meaning to, without even trying.

I closed my eyes and waited, frozen in place, thinking of the deep furrows I'd seen in the door at the top of the tower, and how my tender flesh was no match for that hard wood.

Something warm wrapped around my shoulder and I opened my eyes to see that he was human now, standing before me, studying me with those intense golden eyes.

I had just enough time to take in the huge, muscular form and the attendant gasps of the other women in the circle.

Then I was being ripped from the ground and thrown over his shoulder.

"Cori," Lark cried out from her place beside me.

But we were moving fast, too fast for her to stop him, even if she'd had the strength.

And she didn't. No one did. He was incredibly strong. No one had lifted me up since childhood. I was sensitive about my size.

But the guardian moved with me as if I were an afterthought.

In the span of a breath, we were inside again, paintings and doorways flashing past. Even upside down, over his shoulder, I knew where I was and where he was taking me.

The tower.

7

REED

I took the stairs to the tower two at a time, the girl's satisfying weight over my shoulder, her curvy bottom so close to my face that it was hard to put one foot in front of the other.

All I wanted was to pull her down and claim her here on the stairs, making the whole tower echo with her cries.

But I buttoned my lip and kept moving, finally pushing open the heavy wooden door and closing it behind us.

We were alone in my room at the top of the tower. I eased her gently to the ground, hoping I hadn't frightened her too much.

She clung to my upper arms instinctively and something broke open in my chest. She knew. She knew I would protect her and keep her safe.

Her scent was so luscious that it was almost addictive.

"Cori," I murmured, mesmerized.

"You know my name," she said softly, looking up at me.

Her eyes were wide and frightened. She let go of me and looked back at the ground, hands by her side, as if she were trying not to take up space.

"You have nothing to be afraid of," I said a little too loudly.

She flinched and took an involuntary step back.

Mates weren't supposed to do that. She was supposed to feel my devotion across the bond. I knew she sensed it, but she probably had no idea what it really meant.

"I'm the one who is supposed to protect you," I said, pacing away from her so she wouldn't see my frustration. "You have nothing to worry about from me. I just had to get you out of there before all those witches started prattling."

She made a small, strangled sound and I spun on my heel to look at her, praying that she wasn't crying. Brute as I was, surely I couldn't screw this up that badly. She had been my mate for all of three minutes and I hadn't even claimed her fully yet.

"Those are my friends and my teachers," she protested. But her eyes were twinkling. That sound she had made was a giggle.

Relief washed over me, and I grinned at her like an idiot.

"You're right, though," she went on. "They'll be talking about this for weeks. So do you want to tell me what this is all about?"

I stared at her stupidly.

"Is this something to do with Bella and Luke?" she asked. "Did they find a clue about the Order and the missing page?"

"You know what the Choosing Ceremony is about, right?" I asked her, choosing my words carefully.

Luke's mate, Bella, hadn't known what she was getting into when Luke claimed her. But Bella had arrived at school the day of the ceremony. This girl had been here long enough to know.

She blinked at me, opening her mouth and closing it again.

"Are you... are you *claiming* me?" she asked at last.

"Not if you don't want me to," I assured her, as the beast roared in my chest in protest.

I paced away from her again, trying to soothe it and myself. Everything about being alone in this room with her was driving me wild. Didn't she feel it too?

"Why did you choose me?" she asked. "How did you know you wanted me?"

I stopped pacing and turned to her.

"Of course I knew I wanted you," I growled. "I knew it the minute I saw you."

Her eyes widened and I stalked closer, unable to help myself.

"It's been hell waiting for the moon to come," I told her. "I know you feel it too. You came to me last night. I almost broke down the door to get to you."

Her eyes moved to the door and then back to mine.

Every instinct told me to stop this strange conversation by taking her. But I locked down my desires. No matter how desperate I was to claim her, I knew it was best to be patient and gentle.

Her eyes softened and I prayed for strength.

8

CORI

My heart pounded as I lost myself in those warm golden eyes.

There was something intense and broken about the big shifter. I wasn't wrong to be afraid. He was different from Bella's Luke. There was something more… feral about him.

But he wouldn't harm me. I was sure of it.

He wanted me to be his mate.

I closed my eyes against the images that flashed in my mind of what it would be like to be pinned under that big, gorgeous body. My insides clenched and I felt like a band was tightening between us, pulling me closer to him.

I shivered and wrapped my arms around myself.

"You're cold," he said. "I'm so sorry. And you must be hungry. Let's get you warm and fed."

He moved away from me before I could answer, so I followed him to the kitchenette on the far side of the big round room.

It was basically a very ancient, very charming, studio apartment, with views out over the hills from every window.

The stone walls were exposed, which made it chilly, but otherwise it was a pleasant space.

Though it was nearly empty.

A big mattress on a rag rug next to the kitchenette was covered in furs and pillows and there were a couple of worn paperbacks and a duffel bag on the floor next to it.

Otherwise, the tower was bare. I wondered how long he had been here, prowling around, reading and sleeping.

Waiting for me.

It was clean at least. I had to give him that much.

He grabbed a fur from his humble bed and came close to wrap it around my shoulders. It smelled like him, like the forest, with undertones of something spicy.

As I cuddled with the warm fur, he began banging around in the tiny kitchen, coming up with a loaf of bread, a hunk of cheese, and a pan.

"Grilled cheese?" he offered.

"Sounds great," I told him. "My mom used to make that every time I had a snow day."

"What's a snow day?" he asked, throwing a bit of butter into the pan.

"It's when there's so much snow that people can't drive safely, so they cancel school and sometimes close some businesses, too," I explained, thinking it was weird that he didn't know this. The guardians clearly didn't interact with the outside world much.

"That sounds inconvenient," he guessed.

"For adults it is," I told him. "But kids love it. They get to stay home and play all day instead of going to school."

"I see," he said, smiling. "Snow won't get you out of school here, though."

"No," I agreed. "When you live at school, you don't get snow days. Nothing interferes with Primrose Academy."

"Your parents must be very proud of you," he said.

"Actually," I admitted, "they don't know I'm here."

"Why not?" he asked.

"I don't know," I said, thinking about my normal parents in their normal house. "I guess it just seems like it would be... too much for them. They're super ordinary. They kind of revel in not standing out."

He nodded, but his brow was still furrowed.

"Also, there were some weird incidents from my childhood that my magic might explain," I said. "And they probably wouldn't like it."

"What incidents?" he asked.

"Just some things involving the weather," I told him, not wanting to get into it.

"So it's true?" he asked. "You have weather magic?"

"In theory," I said, ducking my head down. "But all I can do with it is cause problems."

"Don't do that," he said. His voice was closer than before, and deeper.

I looked up.

"Don't be cruel to yourself," he said gruffly. "The greater the power, the harder it is to wield."

"That's what they tell me," I said, shrugging. "But it doesn't change the fact that all I can seem to do is smash up the statues around here."

"I smashed up a statue tonight," he offered.

"That's right, you did," I said, feeling more cheerful. "I think it was the same one, actually. So we have that much going for us, at least."

"So beautiful," he murmured. "I love your smile."

I melted a little. It sounded like a cheesy pick-up line, but he was being sincere. I could actually *feel* it.

Could this be it? Were we actually meant to be together?

An acrid scent filled the air.

"Shit," he said, returning his attention to the stove.

I watched as he expertly flipped our sandwiches in the sizzling pan. They were slightly burnt on one side now, just like my mom used to make them.

"I can actually cook, I promise," he grumbled.

"That makes one of us," I told him. "My parents were more interested in getting me to do school activities."

"That's really nice," he said, looking down at our sandwiches.

There was something melancholy about him for a moment, a flash of sadness in the midst of all that warmth and wildness.

"Did your parents teach you how to cook?" I asked instinctively.

He shook his head. "The guardians took me in when I was little. Every guardian has to be able to fend for himself."

"So you can rough it in the wilderness and all that, too?" I asked, sensing that he didn't want to talk about childhood, though he had definitely stoked my interest.

"Of course," he said. "I wouldn't be much of a guardian if I couldn't go on patrol for weeks at a time."

"You go on patrol for *weeks?*" I asked.

"We typically take shifts," he said. "But in a pinch, yes. I can go on patrol for as long as it takes."

He got a strange look in his eyes that reminded me of the bear.

He *was* the bear, I reminded myself. He was actually a bear, not just a man. The idea of it was thrilling and elusive.

There was a clatter as he put a plate down in front of me that brought me back to the present.

"Eat up while it's warm," he advised me, eating half his sandwich in a single bite, as if to demonstrate.

I took a nibble. It was delicious, so I took a real bite, closing my eyes and savoring it. If this was what he could make with the odds and ends around here, he was probably a world class chef in a fully stocked kitchen.

When I opened my eyes again, he was staring at me, steamy intensity in his golden gaze.

Everything in me turned as gooey as the melted cheese, and I felt the bond tighten around us again, a delicious wanting so deep it was like pain filled the inches between us. I wanted to climb over the counter and wrap myself around him, anything to assuage the yawning ache.

"I want to see you in the moonlight," he growled.

My sandwich hit the plate, forgotten.

He leaped effortlessly over the counter and took my hand, pulling me toward the nearest window.

Pale moonlight poured in, painting the floor in a luminous rectangle. I stepped into it, placing my hands on the stone sill to gaze out over the forest.

Then he was behind me, his hands on the sill, just outside of mine, arms around me, caging me in place.

Heat poured off him and the scent of pine needles and spice filled my senses. He nuzzled my hair and shivers went down my spine. Everything in me sang out for his touch.

One of his big hands wrapped around my hip now, pulling me to him, molding our desperate bodies together.

He was going to claim me and I wasn't afraid. I craved it more than I had ever imagined wanting anything before.

My mind rebelled. I had just met him…

"I-I don't even know your name," I murmured, convincing my mouth to obey my brain somehow.

"Reed," he growled into my hair.

The starry night sky over the trees was fading from me

now, the world was narrowing to Reed and his hands and mouth.

"Fuck," he groaned, dropping his hand from my hip and straightening. "What's that?"

I blinked in confusion, my body still in a haze of lust.

He pointed out the window to something in the distance. I had to look for a moment before I spotted it. In a distant clearing in the middle of the woods there was a tiny red flickering.

"Looks like a campfire," I murmured.

"Watch it," he said.

I watched in silence for a moment, trying to keep my attention on the distant light and not the heat pouring off Reed in waves. It didn't take long to see what he meant.

"It's moving," I whispered.

There was a sudden rush of air as the warmth around me vanished. I turned from the window in time to see Reed's back as he disappeared out the door.

"Stay here," he called out, the sound echoing in the stairwell.

I stood in place, unsure what else to do as the thunder of his footsteps on the stairs faded away from me.

9
REED

The forest crashes past as I fly for the clearing, paws digging into the loamy soil with each heavy stride. I'm disturbing the smaller animals and drawing too much attention, but even my human side can't be unhappy about that. This is not the time for stealth.

There's something in the woods that doesn't belong. And I don't just have the Library to protect now, I have my mate.

This is the other side of the coin. Her presence brings me white hot pleasure and a sense of home. But the thought of her in danger fills me with fury and the soul-deep pain of my human side sings in harmony with my anger.

I haven't felt this range of emotion before. It's dizzying.

But there is no time to feel. I am a creature of action.

If I love this woman, I will show her my devotion by swiftly destroying anything that threatens her.

A night bird cries out and dark wings move before me. I am closer now. I can sense it. The wind changes slightly and the rhythm of my paws on the cold ground falters.

The air carries a smoky scent of brimstone.

I shake myself, my pelt whipping in the night air. I will not *surrender to my fears when Cori's life could be in the balance. This forest is my territory. Nothing can challenge me here.*

The human pushes toward the surface, calling to me, but I press on. He can't traverse the forest with the same reckless abandon I can. He may be larger than ordinary humans, but his flesh is weak compared to the half-ton of muscle and thick fur that protect me from the harsher side of the forest.

I blast through trees and foliage, not even trying to find the thinning areas that could resemble a trail. There's a straight line between me and whatever's happening out there, so that is the direction I will run.

But there's smoke on the air now, growing stronger. I huff it out of my muzzle but more of it greets me on my next inhale.

The forest is burning.

Fear sends shockwaves through me and the human calls to me again, more insistently this time.

I push through to the last of the trees between me and the clearing and then let go.

10

REED

The colors of the forest deepened, and my other senses faded.

The bear normally didn't let me burst through quickly enough to perceive those changes so intensely. I blinked back into my own body as if I were a newborn.

I could still smell the smoke on the air, but I forced myself to stay calm as I stepped between the last few trees into the clearing.

A single column of smoke rose into the air.

Below it, an enormous tree was wrapped in a living gown of flames. The huge canopy of the mighty oak was alight, heat pouring off it that I could feel even from where I stood.

But the scent was all wrong. It wasn't the rich redolence of a normal wood fire.

No. I smelled sulfur again. This was something darker.

For a moment I was frozen in place, overwhelmed at the sense memory that fire always raised in me, the sadness of the mighty oak in flames, and the horrible mystery of that all-wrong scent.

This was three kinds of evil, obviously the result of a deadly mischief.

But whoever had wrought it was gone, I could sense no trace of them, though they had surely been in this clearing not so long ago.

I closed my eyes and pushed my senses outward, looking for life beyond the natural forest life ahead of me, beyond the tree, in the direction they must have fled.

I pushed past the shimmering heartbeats of birds and small mammals, past the low thrum of rabbits and the pounce of a fox.

Suddenly, I sensed movement from the opposite direction.

Someone was running for the clearing.

I turned to meet the intruder, the bear dancing dangerously close to the surface.

11

CORI

Reed turned on me as I stepped into the clearing, his eyes flashing with fury.

"What are you doing here?" he roared.

I stepped back instinctively.

There was pain in his eyes along with the anger. I couldn't understand it.

"Y-you left me," I stammered stupidly. "What was I supposed to do?"

Before he could answer, there was movement in the trees behind me. I turned to see Headmistress Hart and a few of the teachers hustling into the clearing. Even Professor Sora was there, panting, a stray leaf in her silver bun.

"Stand back, Cori," Headmistress Hart yelled out. "Ladies, let's put this out."

Professor Waita trotted to the front, arms out in front of her sturdy body, already reciting a spell in her firm dry voice.

I assumed the magical botany professor was trying to give the tree strength, but it was a spell I had never seen before. I tried my best to follow her words and movements, but I was out of my depth.

"Sora," the headmistress cried out. "Help me freeze it out."

The tiny magical theory lecturer joined Headmistress Hart, their physical types so different, but their magic in perfect synchronization.

I watched as a pale mist left their hands, floating toward the tree's flaming branches.

But it had no effect that I could see.

Silas Brake, the groundskeeper and the only man on staff at Primrose Academy, jogged up with a shovel over his shoulder, panting raggedly.

He began to hurriedly dig in the loamy soil just outside the heat of the burning tree.

Professor Batts said a spell over him, and his work sped up, the shovel flying through the moist soil with and almost eerie quickness.

Students began appearing on the edges of the trees as the professors worked to stop the flames.

"Are you okay?" Anya asked, jogging up to me.

"Sure, it's just..." I looked for Reed, but he was gone. He must have slipped away when all the witches showed up. "Sure."

"Did he do this?" Anya asked.

"No, no of course not," I told her. "I, uh, also didn't do it."

"Obviously," she said.

But it wasn't obvious. I messed up literally everything I touched. If I had real control of my magic, I could make it rain right now, put out that fire, and save the day.

But I would more likely strike it with lightning or cause it to hail directly on the headmistress, or literally anything other than help.

Anya would say I was being too hard on myself, but my shortcomings were made painfully clear by the fact that no one had even asked me to help.

"Did he... did you?" Anya asked. I could see her mind working at finding a polite way to phrase her the real burning question on her mind.

"No," I said. "We had a grilled cheese sandwich, and then we saw the fire out the window, and he just took off."

"Wow," she said.

"I followed him," I said, remembering the fury in his eyes. "But he wasn't happy to see me here."

"Well, his whole deal is that he wants to protect you, right?" Anya asked.

I shrugged, feeling dejected.

"He's supposed to be your *Lord Protector*, idiot," she said, giving me a friendly shove. "He obviously doesn't want you out at night in the middle of a potential forest fire."

"He didn't say that," I told her.

"I got the impression earlier that he's not really a big talker," Anya said, quirking an eyebrow.

He had lumbered out of the castle as a bear and transformed into a man only to throw me over his shoulder and run to the tower. She wasn't wrong.

I grabbed her hand and squeezed it. Anya was a good friend.

We turned back to the tree. Silas had dug a trench in a half circle around the wide trunk. Which was impressive, since the tree was massive. It looked as old as the one in the center of the library. He stepped back as Professor Merness raised both her hands to the heavens, singing something too softly for me to hear over the jumble of other sounds.

At first it seemed that nothing was happening. But then I

realized water was bubbling up out of the ground to fill the trench, turning it into a sort of moat.

The professors moved to the edge of the water and I watched in wonder as they raised their hands as one, chanting and swirling until the water formed a mist that enveloped the tree.

The headmistress leapt forward, vaulting herself over the moat and into the fiery oven-like heat that surrounded the tree. I could feel it even from back where we stood, and for the first time I was really afraid for her.

But Headmistress Hart clearly wasn't afraid at all. The fire shone in her ebony hair and lit her face so that she looked like a goddess from an ancient myth.

A cool blue glow emanated from her palms, growing slowly and then picking up speed until she appeared to hold an enormous ball of shimmering blue magic.

She released it and it floated like a bubble on the night air, up, up to the top of the tree.

Headmistress Hart clapped her hands together over her head and it burst, sending a deluge of magic down over the tree as the others continued the flow of the mist, swirling it all around her.

The flames convulsed, as if the fire itself were alive and fighting against the magic. But the combined force of the witches of Primrose Academy was too much. It sputtered and went out.

The clearing went up in a cheer as students and staff celebrated saving the forest.

Headmistress Hart swung around to face us all from the other side of the moat.

"Well done, women," she called out, her deep contralto ringing across the meadow. "The fire is no longer a danger, but this is a time of loss. This was the oldest tree in the forest, and now it's nothing but ash."

Her words seemed to echo in my mind. There was something so familiar about them.

It hit me.

The page from Bella's book - it was full of components for the spell the warlocks from the Order of the Broken Blade were convinced would bring back the Raven King. Lark and Nina had translated it so that we could have some idea of what the warlocks would be after, and do our best to keep them from it.

One of the things we'd told Luke and the other guardians to keep an eye on was the oldest ash tree in the forest. They had narrowed it down to a few and sent guardians to patrol those areas in shifts.

But we'd had it wrong. It wasn't *the oldest ash tree*.

I glanced over at Anya. She was looking at me too, eyes widened slightly.

Lark and Nina had joined the gathering at some point. I noticed them looking our way and whispering to each other, clearly coming to the same conclusion I just did. Kendall broke from the crowd and began making her way over, leaving Esme and Dozie gazing after her.

"It's *ash from the oldest tree*, isn't it?" Kendall demanded as she reached us.

"Hush, Kendall," Anya hissed, looking over her shoulder, as if that meant anything to anyone but us.

We needed to tell the guardians about our mistake. I glanced around again for Reed on pure instinct, knowing he wouldn't go far from me.

After all, I'm supposed to spend three nights in his bed.

12

CORI

Relief washed through me as I sensed Reed's approach. He really hadn't gone far. Probably just out of view of the professors, who, along with the rest of the gathering, had abandoned the clearing at this point, leaving just me and my friends at the scene.

"Cori." Reed's voice was rusty, as if from disuse.

Anya's eyes widened and the others took a step back.

I turned fully toward him, forgetting how tall he was and coming face to face with his mighty pecs.

I lifted my gaze slowly to meet his golden eyes.

"I told you to stay in the tower," he roared. "It's dangerous out here."

He was shouting at me in front of my friends. Humiliation threatened, but I tamped it down, deciding to get angry instead.

"I'm the most dangerous thing out here," I told him coldly.

"Don't be ridiculous," he sputtered.

"Then don't patronize me," I said. "I don't need a babysitter."

I turned on my heel, expecting my friends to be super impressed with the way I handled him.

But they were all slinking away like he'd just caught us shoplifting or something. Anya gave me a weak, half-wave as she turned away and headed back toward the school. I didn't blame her. I kind of felt like doing the same thing.

"I'm just looking out for you," he said in a voice so calm I was very sure he wanted to kill me. "That's what guardians do."

"We should gather some of that ash," I told him, deciding not to indulge his bad behavior.

"I want you home, *now*," he said.

I ignored him, marching toward the moat as if he didn't matter at all. But I was secretly relieved to feel the rhythm of his footsteps stalking up behind me.

On top of the normal burned wood, the scent of sulfur floated on the air. It grew more noticeable as I drew closer to the trench.

"What are you doing?" he asked.

I gathered up my skirts, took a deep breath, and jumped across the dark water, landing on the other side in a crouch. By the grace of God I didn't slip on the mud and fall into the moat butt first.

I headed up to the smoldering black skeleton of the oldest tree in the forest. Behind me, I heard Reed's massive form hit the ground on the other side of the moat, somehow making less noise than I had.

He was sticking close to me.

I smiled, in spite of myself.

Hold it together, Cori. Do what you came here to do.

But as I approached the tree, I realized I didn't have any kind of vessel.

"We were wrong," I said plainly. "The Order of the

Broken Blade was after ash from the oldest tree. And now they have it."

I hurriedly scraped some of the ash from the trunk and dumped it unceremoniously into the pocket of my gown. It was unscientific and smelly, but I needed to get the ashes back to my friends so we could talk about the spell and what to do next.

"Why are you so mad at me?" Reed growled from behind me.

I spun around, frustrated with both of us now.

"You just yelled at me in front of my friends," I shouted.

He opened his mouth and closed it again.

"You shouldn't yell at me at all," I went on. "If I'm your mate, aren't you supposed to cherish me?"

"If I'm your mate, aren't you supposed to trust me?" he growled, stalking closer. "I told you to stay in the tower for a reason."

"How can I trust you?" I demanded. "I barely know you. All I know is that you're loud and bossy and embarrassing."

I had crossed a line somehow. The air went cold between us and I could see his eyes go from warm honey to flashing white gold.

"You have only three nights to spend with me," he said coldly. "And one of them is already done."

He pointed to the pale pink of the horizon where the sun was beginning to rise.

I felt a pang of pain in my heart. Hot tears prickled my eyes though I didn't know why.

I buttoned my lip and marched past him, back toward the school.

13
REED

I made my way slowly through the woods as the sun reached its highest point, adding just a hint of warmth to the cool autumn day.

My human form usually felt too weak and sluggish for a trek through the forest, but I needed time to think as a man.

The bear relied on sounds and scents, but focused less on what he could see. The forest seemed almost new to me, now that vision was my strongest sense.

Fallen leaves sparkled in the sunlight that filtered through the canopy to illuminate the tiny, dewy puddles in the leaves below. The soil beneath my feet was dark and lush. Even the tree bark took on more dimension, and I noticed face-like arrangements among the knots and branches here and there.

Was this the way the world looked to my brothers? To my mate? Did they always experience life at this dreamy pace?

I cast my mind to Cori and tried to imagine things from her perspective, everything unfolding with majestic slowness.

But I still couldn't fucking figure her out.

I was her mate, sent by fate to protect and pleasure her. She was my mate, sent to love me.

But I had already failed to protect her in a crux. And she had shrugged off my concerns as if they were a mere annoyance.

The pang of her rejection cut bone deep.

At last, I reached Luke and Bella's cottage. The whole place emanated a homey glow of satisfaction. It made me want to punch Luke in his handsome mug.

I knocked on the door before I could lose my nerve.

"Reed," he said, his eyebrows lifting.

He wasn't used to seeing me wandering the woods in human form. Nobody was.

"Hey, man," I said. "Can we talk?"

"Sure, sure, come on in," he said, recovering and stepping backward to let me inside.

I went over to the crackling fireplace and made a show of warming my hands, even though I wasn't cold. It was awkward to come here to talk and ask advice. I had no idea where to start.

"What's up?" Luke asked lightly.

"We're stretched too thin," I told him, chickening out and talking about the missing page instead. That was much easier than talking about Cori. "We screwed up last night. That tree was the ash they needed, not an ash tree at all, just ash from the oldest tree."

Luke shook his head and sighed.

"We don't even know what half the things are on that list," he agreed. "It's hard to guard stuff you don't know anything about. But I know Bella and her friends are working on that."

"Even if we knew about all of it," I said, "there aren't enough of us to keep an eye on a list of items that long."

"We don't need to keep an eye on all the things," he replied. "Just the rare ones."

"They already have the rarest," I muttered.

"Jared," he said on an exhale.

We both went silent for a moment, thinking about our lost brother in arms. The panther shifter had gone missing almost two years ago. I felt his absence every day.

Our kind were slow to form bonds, other than the mate bond. And we were slow to let go too. The pain of losing one of our own had very nearly torn us apart.

"We tried," Luke murmured.

I nodded. We had tried. The search had been dangerous and long. At first, some of the other guardians believed Jared had run. But Luke and I knew better.

We didn't give up the search officially until a year had passed.

And I didn't know if Luke knew it, but I still searched for clues.

At this point, I knew we would have heard from him if he had run, which meant he had been captured by the Order of the Broken Blade. And the Order would not have kept him alive.

Some of the guardians worried that Jared might reveal our secrets under pain, but I never gave that a thought. Our friend would have been loyal until the end.

I hoped at least to find his remains and bring them home to the guardians one day. It was the least I could do for my brother.

The big panther had always been kind to me. He would have known how to help me with Cori.

"How's it going with the girl?" Luke asked knowingly.

"Awful," I admitted. "I actually came here for advice."

"Better come back when Bella's here," Luke said, looking a little alarmed.

"I came because she's *not* here," I told him. "How am I supposed to do this, man? She's *so* mad at me."

"What did you do?" Luke asked in a reasonable tone that made me want to tear his house apart.

"Nothing," I retorted. "I tried to keep her safe and she ignored me."

"She didn't ask for this," Luke said carefully. "Until last night, she looked out for herself."

"I didn't ask for this either," I said. "And the worst part is having to be human so much of the time. You know I don't like being human. And she doesn't want to be mated to an actual bear."

"You came here today as a human," he said, frowning thoughtfully.

"So we could talk," I hedged.

"You walked through the woods as a human," he said.

"How did you know?" I demanded, frustrated to have been caught.

"You have, um, forest stuff on your clothes," he said politely.

I looked down at myself. I was covered in leaves, pine needles and mud. I had tracked it all over his previously clean house.

"Sorry, man," I said. "I guess I'm really not used to being in this form that much."

"You don't like spending time as a human because you've never met a human worth spending a lot of time with," Luke said quietly. "But I think that has changed."

I whipped around to look at him, but he was studiously

brushing invisible dust off his sleeve with one of his big hands, leaving me with nothing to do but think about what he had said.

I exhaled loudly and marched back out his door without saying goodbye.

14

CORI

I piled food on my tray absentmindedly, thoughts of Reed and mate bonds filling my head, leaving no room for something as mundane as lunch.

I'd spent the whole morning in a stupor, unable to concentrate on my lecture class, bumbling into people as I traversed the halls. It would be good to talk with my friends over lunch, maybe pull myself back into the present.

I stepped out of line, tray in hand, and spotted them the big table in the back corner of the cafeteria.

Anya and Bella were on one side with an empty seat left for me. Across the table, Nina and Lark chattered excitedly. There was an empty seat on their side that Kendall might or might not fill.

Kendall was tall, blonde, athletic, and a member of the exclusive group of popular girls who called themselves legacies or "legs" because their parents were alumni of Primrose Academy.

She was in Bellwether house, just like Anya, Bella and me. And she had pledged herself to our cause, stopping the

Order of the Broken Blade from using their stolen spell to wake the Raven King.

It was a big commitment, but Kendall still seemed to float between groups, as if she could be one of us and one of them at the same time.

"How's it going?" Bella asked as I approached. Her long, dark hair was pulled back and her deep blue eyes were filled with concern.

If anyone understood what was happening to me, it was Bella. She'd gone through it all herself, only a month ago.

"I'm... overwhelmed," I said, sitting down beside her.

"It will get easier," she said, putting a comforting arm around me. "But your life has changed. The sooner you can accept that, the sooner things will start to feel normal."

The rest of the table had gone silent as everyone listened. It was weird to be the focus of all this attention. But I didn't care enough for it to stop me from talking to Bella.

"Do things feel normal to you?" I asked her.

"Not really," she said with a smile. "Not yet. But they feel *right*. Does that make sense?"

I nodded.

"Yeah, it does. You got a good one. Luke is super nice."

"Reed is his best friend," she told me in solemn voice.

"He's bossy," I said dismissively. "He treated me like a child."

"That's their whole deal," she told me. "It's not personal. That's just his natural instinct bubbling up, demanding that he protect you. It's what he's been training for his entire life. Try to be sympathetic."

I nodded, but I couldn't help but think about him yelling at me in front of my friends like I was a naughty toddler.

"Are you guys getting anywhere with the list?" I asked, ready to change the subject.

"Clearly we got the part about the ash wrong," Nina said, shaking her head.

"We were pretty close on that though," Lark said, straightening her purple cat-eye glasses. "And we're making progress with some of the other items."

"Even if we figured out every one of them, there just aren't enough guardians," Bella said quietly. "Luke and I were talking about it, and he says it's going to be very difficult to stop them."

I thought about that. Our current plan was to identify the items on the list and get to their sources before the Order could. But Bella was right, unless we told the rest of the witches, we wouldn't have enough coverage.

And we would never do that, because it would involve telling them that Bella had taken a book from the restricted section of the Library and spirited it out of the castle.

She was incredibly lucky that the school was allowing her to continue her education even after being mated. Something like that would get her kicked out for sure, and maybe mess up our relationship with the guardians, since they knew and the witches didn't.

"Even if we told the witches, there wouldn't be enough," Anya said, clearly thinking along the same lines I was.

"We can't let them bring back the Raven King," Nina said. "I've been reading a lot about the fae. Bringing down the veil would be disastrous for humanity."

"There has to be a way to fix this," Bella said. Her voice was pitched slightly higher than usual, the tension in it palpable.

"It isn't your fault," Anya told her. "If you had known what could happen, you wouldn't have taken it."

"You'd only been here a few days," Lark added. "We just have to stop the spell. And we will, somehow."

Stop the spell.

"My God," I breathed.

"What's wrong?" Anya asked.

"In Sora's class, she was talking about how to stop a spell," I said. "The best way is what we're trying to do - stop it before it happens."

"Right," Bella said.

"But if you can't do that," I said, "then you can do a spell that opposes it, like ice to stop fire."

"Like the professors did with the tree," Bella noted.

"But there is no spell to put the raven king to sleep," Nina said. "At least none that any of us could perform."

"What about a counter spell?" I asked.

Everyone was quiet for a minute.

"We'd have to gather all the same materials," Anya thought it through out loud. "But at least we wouldn't have to stop the Order at every turn."

"We'd need to be able to actually do the spell," Lark said.

"Anya never messes up a spell," Bella pointed out.

"How would we know when they plan to cast it?" Anya asked.

Damn. That was a good question. We couldn't cast a counter spell unless we knew exactly when the actual spell was happening.

"There are some guidelines in the spell," Lark noted. "Stuff about the conditions for casting. I bet if we put them all together, it would tell us the best time and place to perform the ritual. And the Order would definitely shoot for the ideal casting conditions to maximize their chance of success."

So maybe we were actually onto something here after all.

"We'd need to figure out all the clues," Nina added,

looking down at her notebook, where she had already reassembled the list.

"Let's each pick an item," Anya decided. "We'll work on the clue and then try to retrieve the item."

There was an excitement at the table, a sense of renewed hope.

I bit my lip and tried not to grin.

"Nice thinking, Cori," Lark said, winking at me from across the table.

I wasn't exactly a good student, or a respected witch. But I had just come up with an idea that might work. Witch pride was an unfamiliar but welcome feeling. I winked back at her.

The others were passing the notebook around, putting their names next to various clues and snapping pictures with their phones. We might not be able to use our phones to communicate with the outside world as long as we were at Primrose Academy, but they still had their uses.

I jotted my name down next to a random ingredient and snapped a pic.

"That's a tough one, Cori," Anya said.

"Reed will help her," Bella said softly.

Nina giggled and Lark joined in.

"Guys, come on," I protested. "It's not like that. We kind of hate each other."

"Sure you do," Lark laughed.

"It'll get better soon," Bella said, waggling her eyebrows at me.

I scowled. I didn't want things to be better with Reed.

But if I could get him to help me solve this clue, and find the ingredient for the spell, that would be nice.

I could get used to feeling like a useful witch.

15
CORI

After my afternoon class, I sat on my bed staring at the ingredient clue on my phone.

Written in cochineal from a source that has never seen sunlight...

I HAD ALREADY LOOKED up *cochineal*. It could be a red dye used for food coloring. Or it could refer to a red pigment created from the shell of a beetle.

The food coloring angle seemed like a long shot. Food coloring wasn't uncommon. Plus I doubted that there would be anything on the list that we could pick up at the local grocery store. And since modern food coloring was produced and kept indoors, why would not seeing the sunlight be important?

No. It had to be the second definition.

But beetles lived outdoors. How could I find pigment from a beetle that lived indoors?

I thought briefly about zoos and aquariums. Maybe even a pet supply shop would have some sort of feeder bugs.

But the spell book predated all that.

So I was looking for an honest to goodness beetle that lived its whole life indoors.

No. Not necessarily indoors - just out of the sunlight.

After a quick trip downstairs and a few quizzical looks, I was back in my room ten minutes later with everything the Primrose Academy library had to say on the fascinating subject of beetles. I cracked open the first book and got down to business.

First, I learned about darkling beetles, but they didn't have scarlet shells. In fact, none of the nocturnal beetles I found seemed to have them.

I threw the book onto my bed and paced a little.

I wasn't looking for a nocturnal insect, not just something that lived under a rock. The forest nearby wasn't entirely dark, even in the thickest parts.

What was I missing?

I pictured the campus, the maze, the woods, the lake below, the cliffside.

"Of course," I said out loud. "A cave."

I searched the indexes for cave beetle and the second book led me to an entry about them. Sure enough, they were long, ant-like, and red.

Jackpot.

I congratulated myself inwardly and pulled on my boots. If we left now, we might make it to the cliffside and back by sundown.

I hustled back down the hallway, ignoring the stares of the other women.

It was probably weird to them that the worst witch at Primrose Academy had been chosen by a guardian.

And to top it off, I wasn't exactly the prettiest girl at school either. I loved my strong, curvy body and my mop of dark curls, but you didn't see a lot of women who looked like me on the covers of magazines.

Reed on the other hand... Reed was beautiful. He was legitimately, over-the-top gorgeous.

I wondered what we had looked like together to everyone.

Then I remembered that he had been a bear when he chose me. So we must have looked like an ordinary woman, and a bear. Which was odd, to say the least.

It was hard not to wonder why he had come to me as a bear.

I shook my head to clear my thoughts as I headed up the stairs of the tower.

The door at the bottom had been unlocked, which was a sign he would be waiting for me. And speaking of signs, the one warning students away was gone. Now that my classmates knew there was a bear in the tower, I guessed the headmistress thought they weren't very likely to go poking around up there.

In any case, I was glad I didn't have to use my magic to get through the door again. I couldn't afford to be confused right now. I had a clear idea of what needed to be done.

The stairs seemed to go on and on endlessly. It occurred to me that the last time I'd been carried up. I'd been a bit embarrassed at the time, but there was something to be said for skipping so many steps.

When I finally reached the top, I knocked on the door.

After only a few seconds, the door opened and Reed stood before me, in man form.

I thought the stairs had taken some of the wind out of me, but the sight that greeted me left me absolutely breathless. Reed wore a pair of worn jeans, and nothing else, leaving his feet and incredible torso bare. His hair tangled around his shoulders in a shaggy mane. His golden eyes blazed.

"You're early," he growled.

I gaped at him for a moment before I could clear my thoughts.

"Stop leering at me," I told him firmly. "You're coming with me."

"Where are we going?" he asked lazily.

"We have to get a beetle out of a cave," I told him. "You know where all the caves are."

"Oh, I see," he said. "Because I'm a bear I know where all the caves are?"

Shit. Was that racist, or… species-ist?

"Well, do you?" I asked.

"Yes, obviously I know where all the caves are," he said, grinning. "I've been a ranger in these woods since I was a teenager."

I rolled my eyes.

"Put on some clothes and meet me at the maze in twenty minutes."

"Sure you don't want to come in first?" he offered in a smooth, golden voice, one eyebrow arched.

My body surged with lust, but I forced myself to turn away.

"Twenty minutes," I yelled over my shoulder as I headed back down the stairs.

My heart was pounding and I had to admit that I was feeling really excited about seeing him again for our adventure. I had to remind myself to slow down and think about the reality of the situation.

He might be super-hot, and he might be attracted to me, but at the end of the day, he was the kind of guy who would yell at me in front of my friends - the kind of guy who thought he always knew best.

My magic might be beyond me at the moment, but I wasn't ready to be anyone's pet.

I had just reached the bottom of the tower stairs and stepped out into the hallway, when someone touched my shoulder, making me jump.

"Cori," Miss Twillbottom's voice was always a bit high-pitched, but today she sounded downright anxious. "Headmistress Hart would like to see you."

"Sure," I said, turning to see Miss Twillbottom scurrying off in the direction of the headmistress's office, an envelope in her hand.

I followed her, wondering what I'd done wrong now. It probably had to do with my make up assignments.

Every time I screwed up a practical, I had to make it up with an essay or book assignment. The professors all said it wasn't my fault, that magic like mine was hard to wield.

But it never seemed to stop them from loading me up with a punishing amount of make-up work.

As the practicals got harder, it seemed like I had more and more writing and reading to do in addition to my regular classwork.

With the Choosing Ceremony, and everything that happened afterward, I hadn't had time to do any of it last night.

I thought my teachers would understand that I would have some late assignments. But clearly they didn't, if I was being rushed off to see the headmistress about it.

Miss Twillbottom threw open the door to reveal Headmistress Hart's office. It was a spacious, yet warm room with a view over the woods.

The headmistress had decorated it with magical items from all the places she had visited when she was a young ambassador of magic. An African world globe, carved of priceless wood, spun on its own in a stand by the window. The bookshelves were covered in ancient editions, magnetic spheres from Finland, a Grecian copper maze, and rows of things I didn't even recognize.

Headmistress Hart herself sat behind an enormous mahogany desk. The desk was like the headmistress, beautiful and inscrutable. You could lose yourself in the depths of the dark polished wood, which offered nothing on its surface to tell you what to expect - just like the headmistress's beautiful dark eyes, which were fixed on me now.

"Hello, Cori, please sit," she said, indicating the chair opposite the desk.

That was the chair where visiting parents sat. Students stood politely, awaiting instruction.

"Go on," she said impatiently.

I pulled the chair out and sat.

"This came for you, Headmistress," Miss Twillbottom quavered, handing the envelope to her, then scurrying out, closing the door behind her.

"Thank you, Regina," the headmistress said, pulling an engraved silver letter opener from the top drawer of her desk.

I waited while she opened the envelope and looked at the letter. I couldn't help but feel it was a bit of a power move - asking me to come here and then making me wait while she opened her mail.

At last, she slipped the letter and opener into her drawer, and finally looked up at me.

"So, Cori, how's it going?" she asked, leaning back as if prepared to wait all afternoon for me to respond.

Great. How was I supposed to answer that open ended question?

"I'm, uh, okay," I mumbled. "Last night was a little intense, so I didn't get to all of my make up work…"

She let me trail off as she observed me shrewdly.

"I'll try to get it all done before the weekend," I added.

"Cori, you have been chosen by a guardian to be his mate," she said, ignoring my bumbling statements. "There have been changes to our agreement with the guardians, as you know. Your friend, Bella is still with us at the school."

I nodded as earnestly as I knew how.

"I wanted to speak with you, Cori, so that you would know, that the changes to the rules do not in any way impede you from making up your own mind," she said.

I blinked at her, not getting it.

"Just because Bella chose to return to school after her mating, doesn't mean you have to," she said plainly. "If that's what you choose."

Ouch.

I nodded as tears prickled the back of my eyes.

She didn't want me here anymore. It didn't matter that I worked harder than anyone else. All my *potential* they always talked about, all work I'd put into trying to control my magic, none of it mattered.

I was a nuisance, a clumsy embarrassment. Maybe even a fatal accident waiting to happen.

Being chosen as Reed's mate might have been lucky. Because it would have stung to be kicked out of school without a reason. If I left with Reed, we all saved face.

"You'll let me know when you decide?" Her voice was light, like she didn't even care what my answer was.

I nodded, unable to speak without crying.

"Good girl," she said, standing. "Don't worry about the make-up work for now. I'll explain everything to your professors."

I scrambled out of the chair and managed to open the door and get out the hallway before the tears started leaking from my eyes.

I was furious with myself for crying. If I'd been able to hold back the tears maybe I could have told her how much I loved being a witch, and how hard I was working to stay.

But I doubted it would matter. Hart seemed like the kind of witch whose powers had always come effortlessly. She wouldn't value a student like me, who tried too hard and wore her heart on her sleeve.

The halls blurred past, and I burst out the door into the courtyard.

Wind whipped at my dress and hair. The sky was gray overhead. Rain wasn't expected, but it looked like it was coming anyway, and right before I was about to go for a hike on the cliffside. I couldn't catch a break today.

I heard the door to the castle slam again and turned back to see Kendall darting off. She must have been looking for a clue too. She didn't even wave to me.

It was like I was already gone.

I kept walking, punishing the cobblestones with my strides in an angry rhythm.

At last I reached the maze. The boxwoods were particularly verdant in the hazy air. That wild green seemed almost unnatural against the contrast of the gray sky. But they didn't catch my attention for long.

Because Reed was there already, waiting for me.

My breath caught in my throat and all my pain and anger fell away. There was only Reed, his golden eyes fixed on mine.

16

REED

There was something wrong.

Cori didn't exactly beam at me most times, but her demeanor was usually so pleasant, so calm. This was something else.

I could feel the anger bristling from her, and the pain in her chest, as if the emotions were my own.

She stopped and looked up at me, and I felt a little of her unhappiness melting away.

I was a grown man, and a half-ton bear most of the time. But I had never felt stronger.

Knowing that she trusted me with her burdens, as a mate should do, even if she hadn't recognized it yet, made me feel like I could move mountains.

"Cori," I growled, unable to think of one other word in the entire language.

She swallowed audibly, another encouraging sign.

Though I wanted to pull her into my arms, I offered her my hand instead. "Are you ready to see the caves?"

She nodded and took my hand. A slight smile curved up the corners of her lovely mouth.

I squeezed her hand as gently as I knew how, nearly shivering at the pleasure of her touch.

"Is it a long walk?" she asked.

"For me? No," I told her, wondering what would be considered normal for most people. I'd been a guardian so long I had no clue.

"More than a mile?" she asked.

"Yes, more than I mile," I told her. "But less than five."

Her eyes widened, but she nodded gamely.

"If it sounds like too much, I can carry you," I offered.

"No," she said quickly. "But thank you anyway. I like going for walks."

"Do you do it often?" I asked her.

She shook her head. "I spend most of my time studying."

"Shouldn't you be spending more time in nature?" I asked. "To encourage your gift?"

"The last thing they want is to encourage my gift," she said, with a bitter smile.

My Cori wasn't a bitter person. I knew this about her already.

"Why not?" I asked, deciding to take her statement at face value. "I would think the school would be proud to have a student with such an illustrious future."

"A future lying around a cave with a bunch of bear cubs?" she asked. "No offense."

"None taken," I lied. Relaxing and playing with our cubs together sounded great to me. I could picture the children already. They would all have my eyes and their mother's incredible hair.

But I could see how she wouldn't want to walk away from her education.

"You do know our whole organization went to bat so that you could have choices after we mate, right?" I added.

"That was really awesome," she said, finally looking up at me with her usual earnest expression. "It meant the world to Bella."

"But not to you?" I asked.

"I don't really want to talk about it," she said, looking down at the ground.

I suppressed the growl that was trying to escape my chest. If she wanted a little space, she should have it. Just because I wanted to bare my soul to her, didn't mean she had to feel the same way. That would happen over time, I hoped.

"So why are we looking for beetles?" I asked.

"Oh, it's one of the ingredients on the page the Order stole," she told me, brightening at the change of subject. "I think we figured out how to stop them."

"We can't be everywhere at once," I warned her.

"We don't have to be," she said, eyes twinkling. "We can do a counter spell."

I stopped in my tracks. "What does that mean?" I asked.

"It means that we can replicate the spell ourselves, but change one key element," she said. "If we do it properly, it will stop the original spell instantly."

"That's genius," I told her honestly. "That changes everything."

"I hope so," she said with a shrug and a half smile.

I could feel the pleasure bubbling in her.

"That was your idea, wasn't it?" I realized out loud.

"We learned about it in a lecture class," she said. "It just hit me that it might work in this situation, and the others agreed."

"You're amazing," I told her honestly.

This time she let herself really smile and I swore I could

feel my heart leaving my body to rest in the palm of her little hand.

17
CORI

We walked until the sun began to sink. It was cold out, but the fresh air smelled clean and pure. It was actually more invigorating than tiring, at least at first.

By the time we got close, I was beginning to feel better, more like myself. A long walk in the woods at twilight with the man who had proclaimed himself my mate was actually doing me good.

I tried to concentrate on the task at hand, but it was hard with my whole body laser focused on the feel of his hand around mine.

We approached a section of the cliff face where there was a break in the foliage just as the setting sun turned into a fireball on the horizon.

"Here," Reed said, indicating something.

I stepped closer to the rocky ledge. An odd little path led down into darkness. I could hear the sound of running water somewhere ahead.

"What's down there?" I asked, afraid of what he was going to say.

"Caves," he said. "One of them has an underground lake, and that's where we're going to find your red beetle."

"An underground lake?" I echoed.

I hadn't expected that. I hadn't really expected an underground anything, to be honest. I was picturing a nice little indention in the side of the mountain, where we would take like two steps inside and then grab a beetle and leave.

"I'll go first," he offered, letting go of my hand to lower himself onto the path.

It was funny how quickly all my bad feelings threatened to return the moment I lost contact with his hand.

I found myself hurrying to join him, even though I wasn't exactly a fan of underground lakes and whatever creepy crawly things might be waiting in that dark crevasse.

He took my hand again and we walked quietly down the little path until it leveled out in front of a small waterfall. We followed the path behind it, and into the rocky interior of a cave.

It was cold inside, and there was a strange scent. I would have expected a moldy smell, maybe even a coppery one. But this was sharp and bright.

Reed wrinkled his nose, which made his handsome face look momentarily adorable. Then he shook his head and we plunged forward into the darkness.

I couldn't see a thing, and the ground was slippery with moisture. Out of nowhere, there was a high-pitched scream. The echo ricocheted around the walls of the cave.

No.

That wasn't an echo. It was more screams.

Reed pulled me to his chest and I buried my face in his shirt as the air came alive around us.

At last, the cave went quiet again.

"What was that?" I asked.

"Just bats," he said. "We scared them. You might have been able to sneak in here on your own, but I think they can sense the bear on me."

"Can you see in the dark?" I asked him.

"Of course," he said. "Oh. You can't, can you?"

"Nope," I said, cursing the fact that I had left to explore a cave without thinking to bring a flashlight. "Give me a sec, and I'll make myself some light."

"By all means," he said.

I closed my eyes and lifted my palms upward.

I was in utter darkness, in an unfamiliar place with Reed. I couldn't risk paying much of a price for this.

I decided to meditate for a moment to earn a touch of magic. Then I would have to keep my light small and efficient.

Breathe in, breathe out, I told myself.

When my mind was a pure wash of comforting darkness, without the slightest pollution of light or color, I began to smooth out the wrinkles of my mood. I pushed away all my fears, hopes and frustrations until the fabric was smooth and light.

I could feel the headmistress's words falling away into the abyss, along with the stack of make-up work on my desk back at the castle. I watched as Reed, waiting for me at the labyrinth, fell away too.

When there were no more distractions, I envisioned lifting the fabric of myself from both sides, sending my consciousness billowing like the parachute we used to play with in gym class back in my regular life.

A sense of peace rippled through me and I knew I had earned enough magic for a small, dim light to accompany me for a short time.

I opened my eyes again to see a walnut-sized golden ball of magic in my right palm.

It gave off enough light that I could see Reed's expression of admiration.

"Beautiful," he said in a hushed tone.

My eyes were caught on his lips. I suddenly wanted to touch them.

"We, uh, we should keep moving," he said gruffly.

I wrenched my gaze from his, embarrassed.

"I want to keep moving so I can get you back to my bed," he added.

I could feel the blood rushing to my face, and I tried to concentrate on the small circle of the cave in front of me that was illuminated by my magic.

The stone walls were sweating beads of moisture. All around us, stalactites and stalagmites gave the appearance of jagged teeth. There were sounds coming from outside my light, rustling and skittering. I was glad I couldn't see what was making those noises.

I tried not to think about what would happen if I were here alone.

"Look, up ahead," he whispered to me.

"I can't see more than about two feet in front of me," I reminded him.

"It's the lake," he told me. "The beetles will be among the rocks on the other side."

"I have to swim across an underground lake?" I asked, horrified.

"No, love," he said with a chuckle. "I'm going to swim across and you're going to ride on my back."

That sounded marginally better. But I was still going to have to get wet. And it was so cold down here.

We continued on for what felt like hours, but was

possibly only minutes. It was so hard to judge anything when I felt so cut off from the outside world.

"Stop," Reed growled suddenly.

I froze in place.

"It was nothing," he said after a moment. "It smells so strange down here that it's throwing me off."

"What *does* it smell like?" I asked as we walked on.

"Hard to say," he said thoughtfully. "These caves flood and dry out, and different animals live in them. The smells change constantly. But I can normally identify them. This is weird, almost like a smell that isn't a smell. Here we are."

My light reflected back at me on the dark water that was nearly at our feet.

"I have to let go for this part," Reed told me.

I realized I was clinging way too hard to his hand and forced myself to release my grip.

The depth of the water was unfathomable. My light was weak, but the reflections helped me see a little better.

The air moved near me and I cowered instinctively, expecting more bats. But when I turned to Reed, I saw he was no longer there.

Or, he *was* there, but he was also a bear.

The creature gazed at me with his golden eyes, and I felt myself smile. I reached out my left hand to touch that thick, soft-looking pelt.

He bent down to butt the crown of his massive head gently into my palm. I giggled and the sound echoed off the walls of the cave.

It was easier between us this way, somehow. Without the hammering pulse of lust, I could appreciate his gentleness.

I hadn't realized that gentle was how I thought of him until now. But it was true. For all his bluster and bossiness, and his excessive muscles, he had been nothing but gentle with me.

I also realized that I genuinely liked him.

And I was standing here with the beast that was always with him, even when I couldn't see it. This side of him was a massive ball of protective instincts, and I could no more blame it for being protective than I could blame it for being a bear. This was its nature. It saw me as family.

Some of the fury I'd felt when he yelled at me began to dissipate. I might not like what he'd done, but his reasons were apparent to me now.

Maybe he could do better now that he knew it upset me.

Maybe I could do better, too.

The bear lowered himself to the floor of the cave and tilted his velvet muzzle up to me, as if to indicate that I should climb onto his back.

I obeyed, as carefully as I could with only one hand, since the other was still cupping my fading light.

Please last until we get out of here, I pleaded with it.

Reed's fur was warm and soft. I had been afraid to rest my weight on him, but once I was seated, I realized immediately that he was so huge he probably barely registered me at all.

His muscles rippled between my thighs as he rose and began to lumber toward the water's edge. I clung to his ruff and closed my eyes, not wanting to watch.

We hit the water with a terrific splash that had me half-soaked even up on his back. He began to swim, pushing the water swiftly with those massive paws.

It was cold, but his warmth was keeping me together. I was just starting to feel comfortable and enjoy the adventure, when something stung my calf.

I yanked my legs out of the water, in too much pain to

scream, and rested them crisscrossed on his back, using my light to examine my injury.

The pain was so intense I expected to see blood. But there was only a strange mark that looked almost like my own blood had been suctioned to the surface of my skin in tiny red dots, forming a strange and almost recognizable shape.

Reed groaned beneath me, and I realized that whatever had done this to me was probably attacking him too.

I turned back toward the shore, but my light wasn't strong enough to show me how far we had come, or how much further we had to go.

I could only see the black water all around us.

Reed moaned again and I lowered my face to his shaggy head.

"I know it hurts," I told him. "Do you have the strength to turn back?"

But he only redoubled his efforts to go forward. I hoped it was because we were closer to our goal than to the shore behind us.

I could already feel his strength flagging, and his body twitching all over from whatever was attacking us.

He was struggling.

And if he surrendered, I would be plunged into the cold, dark water, too.

It occurred to me that I might die here in this underground lake. That wasn't really part of my plan.

"Reed, you can do it," I murmured to him. "You're so strong. Just make it to the other side and we'll figure out how to get out of here."

He had been moving so slowly, but his ears perked up at my words, and I felt his pace pick up slightly.

A few endless minutes later, we reached the island.

He reached for the land, his claws scrabbling for purchase for a moment, and then pulled us out of the water.

I scrambled off his back and held my hand out to examine him with the light.

"Reed, are you okay?" I moaned.

He was limp on the ground, rivulets of water pouring off him. I couldn't see any injuries, but he was so shaggy that it would be hard to spot any markings on him like the one on my leg.

"Reed," I moaned, resting my forehead against his.

The fur beneath me was cold and wet.

And then it wasn't fur anymore.

"Reed," I breathed again, pulling back slightly.

He was in his human form again, his face drawn in pain.

"Get the beetle," he gasped.

The words didn't make sense to me at first. I was so focused on him and the agony on his face.

"If you don't get it, this was for nothing," he groaned.

I moved my hand slowly over his body, but there wasn't a mark on him.

"Go, Cori," he growled.

I scrambled toward the pile of rocks at the center of the little island, smashing my toe against an outcropping I hadn't seen in the circle of my swiftly fading light.

The first rock lifted easily but there was nothing underneath. I hobbled to another and lifted it.

Something skittered out and I snatched it before I could change my mind.

It was a pale red beetle with strange pinchers. Its legs waved frantically, but I had no choice but to wrap a tissue around it and tuck it into my pocket, zipping it up afterward, just to be safe.

I snagged a few more, added them to my zippered

pocket, and then turned back to Reed. He had pulled himself up to a sitting position, but his face was still drawn with pain.

"Did you find it?" he asked.

"I think I got enough," I told him. "Are you okay?"

"I'm fine," he lied. "It's just that my strength is sapped."

"You'll feel better in a bit," I told him. I knew from school that shifters had excellent healing abilities. At least he wouldn't suffer for long.

"I don't know what it is," he said, shaking his head. "I don't have a mark on me, but I'm not healing, either."

So much for that idea.

"We'll wait for help to come, then," I suggested.

"Does anyone know where you went?" he asked.

I sighed.

"No," I said. "Of course not. I'm an idiot."

"That may be for the best," he said gently. "You wouldn't want your friends getting hurt in that water trying to find you. Give me a little time. I'm sure I'll get my strength back."

"You can't go back in there," I said, horrified.

"We have no choice, Cori," he told me. "We can't stay in here forever."

He was right. But I had no idea how we were going to make it out.

"Look," he breathed, pointing to a ripple of movement in the water.

I shone my light, pushing it outward a bit, using up some of its precious energy. I could barely make out the dark outline of something *moving* under the water. Several somethings, actually.

Then my light went out.

18
REED

Her light went out, but she didn't cower or scream.

My own night vision was excellent, so I saw every expression that crossed her exquisite face. For a moment, despair and determination battled there.

And determination won.

Pain still sang through my veins, but my heart was light as I watched my mate rise to her feet and lift her hands, palms up.

I could feel her magic, as if she had sucked something vital out of the air around us and was forming it into... whatever the sparkling glow was that swirled between her hands as if it had a life of its own.

Her dark eyes had gone blue as ice. They glowed like twin lanterns and I felt a fleeting sympathy for whatever had to face off with her now.

I glanced at the water, but it was still roiling with cursed life.

The Order of the Broken Blade had beaten us here. And they had cursed the lake. It was the only explanation that made sense. There was nothing natural about those dark creatures below the surface.

A blast of icy air whipped past me and I turned to my mate once more. But her hands were a blur now.

Winter itself was flying from her, pulling her gown with it, toward the surface of the lake.

I scrambled to my feet just in time to see the lake freeze over.

Holy shit.

Holy fucking shit.

I had seen some of the witches cast spells over the years, but nothing like this. Even the combined powers of the professors as they worked to extinguish the tree hadn't possessed this kind of raw, primal power.

My mate was so powerful that she was practically a goddess.

But when I turned back to her, I could see she was trembling. The effort she was making was palpable. The magic was taking its toll on her.

I grabbed her hand and ran across the ice with her, not quite daring to throw her over my shoulder in case it interrupted the flow of her magic.

Beneath us, the dark things under the ice began to pound against the surface, trying to break through.

"Run, Cori," I told her. "We're almost there."

There was a horrible thud against the ice right under our feet and then a sound like a shotgun crack.

I dragged her, praying I wouldn't jerk her arm out of the socket.

We couldn't let them get to us. Not when we were so close.

She squeezed my hand in hers like a vice and I felt the air go colder still.

At last we reached the bank and scrambled away from the lake until I could see the door sized opening to the cave. We were only a few feet away.

But Cori's hand was cold in mine, and the ice was crawling up the walls of the cave, up to the opening, covering it over, freezing the waterfall that hid the entrance.

"Stop, Cori," I told her. "We're safe now."

But she didn't respond. Her eyes had a glassy, faraway look about them. I didn't think she even knew I was there anymore. And the ice kept surging. It was too much.

I lifted her into my arms and flung her through the last tiny opening in the wall that had once been a waterfall, hoping she made it out on the other side without breaking anything.

I couldn't let her be trapped in here when she ran out of juice and the things in the lake exploded out to express their displeasure.

My heart skipped a beat, but she disappeared on the other side just before the ice closed up behind her.

Alone in the cave, I closed my eyes and waited for the inevitable, trying to gather what little strength I had left.

19
CORI

The world pressed back in on me. I had been... somewhere else. I couldn't remember where.

Now the ground was coming up to hit me.

I was falling.

I landed hard on my hands and knees on a dirt path, in the cold moonlight.

The weight of my own body felt like it was too much to bear. I dragged myself around to see where I had come from, hoping it would bring my memory back.

But I was staring at a wall of solid ice set into a rocky cliffside. I couldn't have come from there.

I could have fallen from the top, but I'd be seriously injured from a fall like that.

Where am I?

I stared at the solid ice and granite trying to piece things back together. Then a crack like the sound of a gunshot brought me out of my thoughts. Splinters of ice flew outward from the wall, and I put up my hands instinctively to protect my eyes.

What's happening?

When I lowered my hands, I saw that something huge stood in an opening in the cliff face that had been revealed when the ice was broken.

A bear. It was a massive bear.

He fixed his feral golden eyes on mine and came at me fast.

I was being attacked by a bear. I was going to die.

I screamed, not knowing if there was a living soul for miles to hear me.

Calling on all my reserves of strength, I reached for my magic, but I could feel that it was depleted. Whatever I had done, it had been a big mistake. And now I was paying the price.

The bear had almost reached me, his eyes were piercing and somehow familiar, even though that didn't make any sense. The breeze ruffled its thick pelt. I wondered what it would feel like when those razor-sharp claws tore me to pieces.

I squeezed my eyes shut and braced myself, hoping it would be fast.

"Cori," a man's voice said softly.

I felt big, warm hands wrap around my shoulders and I shivered with instinctive pleasure as I opened my eyes.

The bear was gone.

In his place was a man with the same fiery golden eyes. He was so handsome I might have described him as beautiful. And he looked worried.

"Cori, are you okay?" he asked.

"I used my magic," I guessed.

"You did," he said.

"I'm paying my price," I admitted. I didn't like making myself vulnerable, but this guy was definitely on my side. I could feel it in my bones.

"What is your price, Cori?" he asked.

"Memory loss," I said quietly, looking down at my hands. "And confusion. I'll get myself back pretty quickly, depending on what I did."

He was silent.

I glanced up to see the tension in his jaw.

"Wh-what did I do?" I asked.

"I can't believe you don't remember," he said. "It was incredible."

"But I screwed it up, didn't I?" I asked, sighing.

"You were amazing," he said. "Why would you think that?"

"Because I always mess it up," I said. "My power is too much for me."

"I don't think so," he said. "You were unbelievable. I wish you had seen yourself."

He reached out to stroke my cheek and I leaned into his hand.

"Reed," I murmured, remembering.

His smile was like a beam of sunlight in a dark forest.

"You remembered me," he said.

"I thought you were a real bear," I chuckled.

"I know," he said. "It's not funny. You were terrified."

"And now I'm cold and hungry," I said, shrugging. "Life goes on."

"And you're soaked," he said, in a tone that implied that he somehow blamed himself. "I have to get you back to the castle."

Back to his bed, I remembered, surpassing a shiver of lust.

"I'm going to shift again," he warned me.

"I won't scream at you this time," I told him. "I definitely remember you."

I watched carefully, but there was only a shimmering

around him as he lowered his head and his shoulders went up in transformation. In a heartbeat, I was face to face with the mountain of a bear once more.

His change seemed painless, effortless. I wondered if it was either.

The bear lowered his body and nodded to me, and I climbed onto his back, grateful that I still had enough energy to do it.

I sank my fingers into that warm, thick pelt and lay my head against his neck, wrapping my thighs around him.

I was too busy luxuriating in his warmth and the delicious forest scent of him to notice when he began to move. One moment I was cuddling into him, the next the trees and foliage of the forest were flying past.

20

REED

I shifted out of my bear form and carried Cori into the castle and up the stairs to the tower as a man, not wanting to terrify any other students we might meet in the halls.

I found myself grateful that we didn't bump into anyone, especially professors.

I might be her intended mate, but how could I justify carrying her home soaking wet on a cold fall night, still dazed from using her magic in such an advanced way without the guidance of a more experienced witch.

Shifters like me had our own magic - the power to change our shapes. But it was inherent in us, present since birth, even if it didn't express itself until later. There was no price for us to pay, our magic was a part of us.

Witches, on the other hand, could wield far more changeable powers. And while the potential was said to be inborn, the practice required careful restraint. If a witch's magic wasn't bought by discipline, it took its own price from her.

I had just allowed the woman I was supposed to protect

to expose herself to the most powerful kind of magic. And she had paid dearly for it.

I thought back to the moment she had screamed in abject terror at the sight of me.

What was the point in having a mate if I couldn't protect her?

She nuzzled my neck as I reached the final landing.

My whole body responded, nearly frantic with lust.

But I tried to fight back my need. I had to understand what I could be to her before I bound her to me forever. I would not be a burden or a pet. That was not in my nature.

I breathed in the sweet perfume of her and exhaled slowly, opening the door to my tower room.

"I'm going to put you in my bed while I start a bath for you," I told her.

She clung to me more tightly, as if unwilling to let me go.

"You're too cold, love," I scolded her gently.

She reluctantly allowed me to lower her into my bed.

I tried not to let myself soak in the sight of her there. But it was impossible not to notice her dark curls spread out on my pillow, her beautiful brown eyes fixed intently on me.

The furs were cool to the touch, but I covered her in them anyway, knowing her own body heat would warm them.

She stretched languorously, instantly inspiring my imagination.

"Give me just a few minutes," I whispered, uncertain how I could resist claiming her when her mere movements had me on a razor's edge.

Maybe she'll fall asleep, I told myself as I prepared a steaming bath. *Maybe if I don't hurry back to her, she'll be dreaming by the time I get there and I can leave her alone until morning.*

Once I had the bath steaming and fragrant with soap bubbles, I walked softly back into the room.

She was sitting up in bed, furs wrapped around her.

"I was afraid I would fall asleep before you got back," she explained, as if she'd read my thoughts.

I could see how pleased she was at having managed to resist sleep for me. My heart was shot through with a love that felt like pain and I stopped in my tracks, uncertain I could bear it.

"Did I do something wrong?" she asked.

"No," I told her. "Let's get you into your bath."

She allowed me to help her up. The furs fell back onto the bed, revealing her gown, plastered to her small, curvy frame.

I sucked in a breath, but it was laced with her scent and my body responded instantly. I paused for a moment, battling my instincts, then took her hand and led her to the bathroom.

"Oh," she said happily as she gazed down at the steaming tub.

She tried to unbutton her gown, but her hands were trembling.

"Let me," I offered. My voice was rough with need, I hoped it didn't frighten her.

She dropped her hands immediately and the bear roared in my chest with satisfaction at this show of submission. I struggled to unbutton the tiny buttons with my big hands, wishing I could rip the thing off her and slam her against a wall.

I could warm her up so fast, she would be panting and sweating with lust...

At last the gown fell in a puddle at her feet, and we removed her undergarments together.

She was exquisite, all dimples and curves, her saucy little nipples hardened into buds.

I wanted to feast on her. I wanted to wrap her in my arms and carry her straight back to bed.

"Let's get you in," I suggested as calmly as I could, taking her hand.

She gazed up at me, her eyes hazy with her own need.

But it only reminded me of her confusion back at the cave. Guilt descended on me, and I forced myself to guide her to the tub and help her step in.

21

CORI

The warm water felt incredible as I stepped in, but I was trembling all over, and my legs felt like noodles.

"Go on, lower yourself in," Reed growled encouragingly.

But I couldn't do it. I wasn't sure if I was weakened from magic, or lust, or both.

"What's wrong?" he asked.

The timbre of his deep voice vibrated inside me and I couldn't speak.

My hand began to tremble in his.

"*Fuck*," he whispered, as if to himself, and let go of my hand.

I almost cried. I didn't want him to leave me. I couldn't bear it.

But he was violently peeling off his own wet clothing, as if he didn't care if he ripped it to shreds.

I watched in awe as he straightened.

His body was beyond anything I had ever seen. His hair tangled down over his shoulders as if it were pointing my eyes toward the swell of his massive pecs and the chiseled abs below. The twin angles of muscle over his hips were set out in sharp relief, and I tried, but failed to ignore his rigid cock.

My belly cramped with need at the sight, even as I ripped my eyes away to meet his golden ones, which stared at me intensely. My cheeks burned with lust and embarrassment in equal measures.

Whatever happened between mates, I was sure it was supposed to be magical and borderline religious - not some useless virgin, struck dumb with lust, gawking at the guardian's junk.

He stepped into the tub and pulled me to him, lowering us down together with my back against his chest.

The water washed over us, and my eyes rolled back with the pleasure of it all.

"Better?" he whispered into my hair, sending a little shiver down my spine.

"Mmm," I agreed, trying to memorize the feel of his arms around me, his chest, warmer than the water...

"Cori," he groaned.

I could feel every inch of him surrounding me, the steel of his wanting, pressed against my posterior as I wiggled against him helplessly, desperate for more.

"Please," he moaned. "Be still. I can't control myself when you move like that."

I tried, I really did, but the hunger in his voice had me arching my back to give him access to my neck.

"Fuck, Cori," he whispered.

My whole body tingled as his lips traced the line of my neck from my ear to my shoulder.

My heart pounded so hard I thought it would jump out of my chest. I longed for the pain of his bite. I had no past, no future, only this moment. I needed to be his.

One of his hands left my waist to cup my left breast. The pleasure was white hot when his thumb brushed my nipple and I cried out.

He growled against my neck and let his other hand join the first at my breasts, toying with me lightly but so expertly that I could feel it between my legs.

"Reed," I whimpered.

He pressed his lips to my neck, his hot breath setting me on fire. My hips were trembling now as I writhed in the warm water.

"Easy, little one," he crooned.

Nothing about this was easy.

"Why don't you want me?" I moaned. I wanted him so much, it wasn't fair.

"Fuck," he cursed again, sliding one hand down my belly.

Normally I was very self-conscious about my curves. I had never been completely naked in front of a guy before.

But with Reed, instead of wanting to pull his hand away from the softness of my belly, I yearned for more. I wanted every part of him to be touching every part of me.

That big, clever hand snaked between my thighs and I moaned at the thought of where he was going.

"Good girl," he growled into my neck.

The first touch of his hand against my sex had me whimpering with pleasure. But Reed was slow and measured, caressing me with teasing touches too gentle to satisfy.

I had touched myself before, but my furtive explorations were nothing compared to the fire he was stoking. I was burning from the inside out, while he toyed slowly with my sex and pinched my nipples between the thumb and forefinger of his other hand.

"Please," I moaned, tilting my hips up shamelessly for more.

He groaned and slid one thick finger slowly inside me, rolling his thumb back and forth over my clit.

I was stretched taut, every nerve laid bare.

He kissed my neck again, allowing his teeth to graze the tender flesh as he worked me faster.

The world seemed to stand still for an instant, and then the pleasure had me flying as I came apart under his hands, sobbing with relief and ecstasy.

22

REED

My mind and body were reeling.

Cori was in my arms, naked and trembling in ecstasy as I fought back the urge to claim her with everything I had.

When her tremors of pleasure slowed, I felt her try to turn to me.

I held her still and closed my eyes to stop myself from imagining what it would feel like for her to close her sweet little hand around my cock.

But if I thought I was going mad now, I knew that would send me over the edge.

And I had already made up my mind. I would not claim her tonight.

The bear moaned with displeasure in my chest, but I ignored him.

"Reed," Cori murmured, her voice low with satisfaction.

I clenched her closer.

"Better?" I asked lightly, hoping she couldn't hear the tension in my voice.

"Mm," she hummed. "But now I want to touch you."

"Gods, Cori," I growled. "It's hard enough for me to hold back."

She didn't reply, and I felt a moment of relief, followed by concern. I didn't want her to feel rejected.

"I want you so much," I told her. "But you can't decide to be claimed when you're hungry and cold and weak from that much magic. I think we managed to warm you up. Now you're going to eat."

She sighed and let her head fall back against me again.

Warmth spread in my chest, knowing I had said the right thing. I only wanted to comfort and please her. I wanted to make her feel safe.

"Okay," she said pleasantly. "I guess I could eat."

"Me too," I told her. I could always eat.

I pressed a kiss to the top of her head and then stood, offering her my hand. The water shimmered as it slid from her body, and I nearly fell to my knees to pleasure her all over again.

But this would not do. I had to get her dressed and fed, so that she could be comfortable again.

I stepped out of the tub and helped her out too, and grabbed each of us a towel. I was dried off and wrapping mine around my waist before she was finished with her hair.

"Take your time," I told her as I grabbed our wet clothes off the floor. "I'll start cooking. You can grab some of my sweats from the shelf."

She glanced over at the shelf that acted as a closet for me and nodded. I made a note to myself that a mate might like me to have nicer clothes than jeans and sweats.

I hadn't ever spent this much time human. Clothes were an obligation, not something I enjoyed playing around with. Maybe Luke could get Bella to help me figure out what Cori would want me to wear.

I hummed as I prepared a midnight snack. I didn't really keep a lot of food around the kitchen, but I had the ingredients for pancakes. And there was honey in the cabinet somewhere. Cori would laugh at me for having it, but I liked it when she laughed.

I was just flipping the last pancake onto a plate when I sensed her coming in.

"Hey," I said, without turning around. "It's just about ready."

"Are you making pancakes?" she asked, padding up behind me.

"Sure am," I told her. "Do you like pancakes?"

"Does anyone *not* like pancakes?" she asked. "Of course, I love them."

She came right up and leaned across the counter to watch as I grabbed silverware, and I got a look at the clothes of mine she'd chosen to wear.

Cori was kind of drowning in my oversized sweats, as if someone had shrunk her. But she had rolled up the pant legs and sleeves to keep them out of her way and she still looked beautiful. I was sure she would be beautiful no matter what she wore.

I put down a plate of buttered pancakes in front of her.

"Do you have syrup?" she asked.

I shook my head.

"Jam?"

"Nope," I told her, letting her have her fun.

"Honey?" she teased, clearly expecting me to say no.

"If I say yes, will you think of me as a bear stereotype forever?" I asked.

"Not if you keep cooking for me," she said, arching an eyebrow.

I grinned and started rummaging around in the cupboards.

"Aha," I said, pulling out the honey with a flourish.

She smiled and watched me release a ribbon of it over her snack and then over mine.

"Cheers," she said, lifting her fork.

I clinked mine to hers, charmed at the silly little show of ceremony.

It was good to be human with Cori. It felt familiar, almost like… family.

"Oh my God, so good," she moaned over her first bite.

I grinned and took a bite of my own stack.

She wasn't wrong. Pancakes were always awesome.

"So, I hate to ask, but where did you put my gown?" she asked.

"I hung it up, but it's going to need laundering," I warned her, pointing to the hooks on the far wall, where our clothing was drying.

"Great," she said, dropping her fork and dashing over to it.

I watched as she fished around in the pocket and pulled out a crumpled bit of tissue.

"Do you have a jar?" she asked.

I blinked at her.

"For the beetles," she said.

"Ah, that makes sense," I replied and banged around in the cabinets until I found a small mason jar that miraculously did have a lid.

"Perfect," she said. "I'm glad I remembered. They might have gotten away."

"You didn't kill them?" I asked, watching her carefully place the tissue inside the jar.

"I wasn't sure if I was supposed to," she said. "Plus it

seemed kind of wrong to murder them unless we have all the other ingredients. We just have to make sure these things don't see the light of day."

"I'll put a piece of apple in there for them, and stick it in the closet," I told her.

"I have to tell the others about this," she said, looking really pumped about it.

"Sure, in the morning," I agreed. "You must be tired now."

"Definitely too tired to go up and down all those stairs," she said. "No wonder you're so buff."

I couldn't help but laugh. Then I strutted around a little, flexing my biceps. She laughed too, and I leaned over the counter and kissed her cheek.

She held very still, and I felt the pull between us, so strong it almost stopped my heart.

"Are you tired?" I asked her.

"I want to go to bed," she said, her voice low and significant.

"Let me take that, then," I told her, grabbing her plate. "You go to bed. I'll be there in a little while."

"I can help clean up," she offered, stifling a yawn.

"No, little one," I told her. "Get in bed."

She smiled up at me and touched my cheek, a featherlight caress that seemed to burn.

Then she padded over to my bed and crawled in.

The bear was exultant in my chest, but I cleaned up the dishes slowly, giving her time to relax.

If I could stay away from her long enough for her to go to sleep, it would be easier to resist.

I just wasn't sure I could manage it.

23

CORI

I woke up warm and happy.

For a moment I luxuriated, eyes closed, then I pulled the blankets up around my shoulders and realized they weren't blankets. They were furs.

I was with Reed.

The events of the previous night flew through my head. The cave, the lake, the beetles, the ice, and then that incredible bath.

He had made me pancakes and sent me to bed.

And I had fallen asleep before he could join me.

I opened my eyes and rolled over slowly, so as not to wake him. I was startled to find him in his bear form, his big furry body half off the mattress and spread across the floor.

He opened one golden eye.

"Good morning," I whispered to him.

I longed to stroke my fingers through that glossy fur, but was afraid it might be insulting somehow. I reached out my hand very slowly.

He butted his forehead against it, making a low chuffing sound. I laughed and stroked his velvety fur.

After a moment, I was stroking hair, since he had shifted under my hands.

"Did you sleep well?" he asked.

I nodded, suddenly feeling shy.

"You should probably get ready for school," he said, sitting up.

"What time is it?" I asked, sitting up, too. But I could see the clock in the kitchen now. "Crap."

I scrambled out of bed and dashed to the door, grabbing my soiled dress from the hook. At least it was dry now.

"I'll, uh, see you tonight," I said.

"What about talking with your friends?" he asked.

"Do you want to have breakfast with us?" I asked him, unbelieving.

"Yes," he said. "Meet you down there in fifteen minutes?"

"Perfect," I told him, heading out the door.

I flew down the tower stairs. Down was so much faster than up. It was sunny outside, warm golden light poured in the windows, reminding me of his eyes.

I was kind of glad to get away from Reed, even for a few minutes. I wanted time to think before I had to face him again. I headed into my room, throwing the gown with my other dirty laundry and grabbing a clean one from my closet.

As I got dressed, I thought about Reed, about us.

Little as I had appreciated him yelling at me the other day, I was starting to understand how much the bear was a part of him. He was making an effort, but he was actually a freaking bear, or half a bear? Either way, it wasn't the same as if a fully human boyfriend freaked out when I was in danger. Reed had instincts that were beyond anything I could imagine. This was different.

For sure, his protective instincts might get annoying at times. But it was also darned handy.

The business in the cave had bled back into my mind, and I knew I wouldn't have made it out without his quick thinking and his drive to protect me.

My magic might have saved us, but he had saved me. He had my back.

And the things he had done to the rest of me in the bath... well, I was still walking on air. I could only imagine what the claiming would be like.

He had even wanted to wait, denying his own satisfaction in order to be sure I wanted him forever.

But I was already secure in my decision. I wanted to be with him. As I walked to the cafeteria, I wondered if me telling him so would be enough. And I tried not to wonder if his hesitation had anything to do with what *he* wanted, not just what I wanted.

I got there before him and grabbed a tray of food. No reason not to go catch up with my friends. They probably had plenty of embarrassing questions that I'd prefer them to ask *before* Reed joined us.

"Cori," Anya called to me, patting the seat beside her.

The whole cafeteria seemed to turn to watch me cross the room. This must have been how Bella felt last month. Having two witches chosen in back-to-back ceremonies had never happened before. It must have the rumor mills working overtime.

"Hey guys," I said, setting down my tray and taking the seat next to Anya.

"Cori," Kendall said, nodding. Our popular, athletic friend had never been overly effusive. At least she was sitting with us today, and not with the other legacy witches.

"How was it?" Anya asked, putting an arm around my

shoulder and fixing me with a concerned gaze. "Are you feeling okay about things?"

Anya might be physically small, but she had big feelings.

I smiled at her reassuringly.

"I'm fine," I said. "It was fine."

Fine. Was that really the word for it? I didn't think so.

"Did you guys...?" Lark asked.

Nina gave Lark a little shove. Nina would never have asked that.

"Ow, don't shove me," Lark scolded, pushing her purple cat-eye frame glasses up her nose. "I'm just asking, not judging."

"Not yet," I told her, trying to suppress a smile.

"But you will?" Anya asked.

"Yeah, I think I will," I told her.

"Oh shit," Kendall said.

I turned in my seat to follow her gaze, expecting something bad, but realizing she was just reacting to spotting Reed. I probably should have warned them that he was going to be joining us.

Reed took up nearly the entire threshold of the cafeteria entrance. He was wearing jeans and a tight white t-shirt that somehow looked more provocative than if he had shown up naked.

I could feel the whole cafeteria take in a collective hormonal female breath, myself included.

Then he spotted me, grinned and gave a little wave.

I melted, just a little, and waved back.

"Wow," Anya murmured.

I turned back around quickly, not wanting to stare at him while he got his breakfast. All the other women would be doing that. He had no lack of admirers.

Bella showed up and sat across from me, placing down a tray with nothing but dry toast and a cup of tea.

"Hey guys," she said.

"Everything okay?" Anya asked, looking at her tray.

"I'm just kind of freaking out," Bella said. "Luke got a tip that campers found something suspicious in the woods. He's going to check it out. I don't like him going without me."

"What did they find?" I asked.

"Hello, Bella," Reed said, sitting beside me.

"Guys, this is Reed," I said. "Reed, you know Bella. Next to her are Nina and Lark. And this is Anya on my other side, and Kendall."

"Nice to meet you all," he said.

There were hellos and nods all around as we all tried not to stare at his plate, which was piled with a mountain of food. It was like something out of a cartoon.

"Did I hear you say Luke was following a lead?" he asked Bella.

"Yes, campers said they saw paw prints up at the bluff," she told him.

"I'll try and catch him as soon as I leave here," Reed said. "Sound good?"

"That would be great," Bella said. She smiled and grabbed a piece of toast, making it clear she actually felt relieved.

It made sense. I couldn't imagine much in the woods that would be too much for Luke and Reed to handle together.

"So, we managed to track down an item from the list last night," I told the others.

"Busy girl," Kendall quipped, arching an eyebrow.

I chose to ignore her. "The clue that says *written in*

cochineal from a source that has never seen sunlight. It refers to ink made from a beetle."

"What beetle hasn't seen sunlight?" Bella asked through her bite of toast.

"A cave beetle," I told her.

"Whoa," Anya said. "You guys went into a cave to find a beetle?"

"It was epic," Reed said, through a massive bite of waffles. "You should have seen Cori."

"It was fine," I said quickly. "We got a few beetles. We need to pick another clue for tonight."

Kendall snickered. She was definitely going to make a sex joke if I didn't cut her off.

"Who has the list?" I asked quickly.

Nina pulled out her notebook and laid it on the table so all of us could see.

"Want to get the white feather from a winter raven?" Reed asked.

"Do you know where that is?" I asked him. "Sounds kind of rare."

"Oh, they are," he said. "There's only one pair in the area. But I know their territory. We'll go tonight."

"It's a plan," I said.

It was fun knowing we were a team. I could feel our bond pulling tighter.

The others went quiet.

I looked around and realized that Reed had very nearly cleaned his plate.

"Well, babe, I gotta go," he told me, standing and kissing the top of my head. "See you after school. It was nice to meet everyone."

"See you," I murmured.

It actually felt like my insides were being pulled out as he loped away past the gaping students.

"I can't believe he just came here and ate breakfast," Lark said dreamily.

"He lives here," I said.

"Yeah, but in the tower," she replied.

"They're going to need more cooks on the morning shift if he keeps eating breakfast with us," Kendall said.

"Big man, big appetite," Nina said thoughtfully, then blanched at the implication.

Nina was pretty much as inexperienced as I was.

Well, as inexperienced as I was before last night anyway.

"I guess we should get to class," I barked out, leaping out of my seat.

I did not want to even think about last night in front of my friends. I swore they could read minds sometimes.

24

REED

The forest was humming with life and the sun was warm on my face. The scent of the morning frost was fading already, giving way to the warmer smells of soil and pine needles.

I missed being out here, missed it a lot, even though I was in human form again today.

I found myself wanting to be in this form lately, even when Cori wasn't near. I felt closer to her this way, I could think more slowly and in more human ways about the complexity of our relationship.

Luke's scent trailed back to me from just up ahead. I jogged to catch up, even as the bond tugged me backward toward my mate. It was a strange sensation, as if she had my heart on a leash.

"Hey, Luke," I called out when I could see the back of his shirt.

"Reed," he cried, turning to wait for me. "I got a tip some campers saw paw prints up on the bluff."

"Bella told me," I said. "She seemed worried."

"Shit," he said. "That's the hard part of this mate business."

"So it's normal?" I asked.

"Who knows?" he said with a shrug. "I only know what it's been like for Bella and me. We're pretty much obsessed with each other."

"That doesn't sound so bad," I admitted.

We walked on in silence for a little while, the birdsong filling in the gap in conversation.

"Do you want to talk about Cori?" Luke asked quietly after a few minutes.

I did. But I wasn't sure how to begin.

"Did you seal the bond?" he asked, as if he knew I was at a loss.

"No," I said. "I'm not sure I will."

"Why not?" he asked, sounding surprised.

"Did you know right away with Bella?" I asked him instead of answering.

"That's complicated," he told me. "I thought I didn't know, but I knew."

That was a non-answer.

"What's holding you back with Cori?" he asked.

"She makes me feel... helpless," I told him.

"Well, that's love for you," he chuckled.

"No, it's not like that," I said, feeling a little annoyed. "I mean literally helpless. We were chasing down one of the items from that spell last night. We got into some trouble, and she saved my ass."

"Sounds like it's not so bad to be helpless," Luke said. "You have an issue with a woman having powers? You should be proud if she's stronger than you."

"First of all, no one is stronger than me," I told him

firmly. "But yeah, her magic is insane. She froze an underground lake."

"That is impressive," Luke said, eyebrows lifted. "Bella kind of gave me the impression that Cori wasn't very good at magic. Please don't share that."

"Of course not," I assured him. "And that's also kind of true. Her powers are incredible. But she needs to grow into them. I watched her pay the price last night, and..." I trailed off. There were no words for it.

"What's her price?" Luke asked.

"Memory loss," I told him. "It's temporary, but it's terrifying. She didn't even know who I was."

"Oh wow," Luke said sympathetically.

"I like her, *a lot*," I told him. "But it scares me that the bond would make her risk herself in that way, to save my sorry ass."

"She's not allowed to like you a lot too?" Luke asked.

"What if she forgets me permanently?" I asked him. "What if she forgets herself because of some trouble I get us into? How can I take a mate, when that bond could risk her mind?"

"Maybe the bond would help," Luke offered.

"What do you mean?"

"What if the bond meant she couldn't forget you?" he asked. "Once you seal it, it's pretty powerful stuff."

I thought about that, but I didn't have an answer. If the bond were any stronger than it was right now, it seemed like we would be able to cross solar systems to find each other.

Or it could drive her insane.

If her heart remembered and her mind didn't, what would that mean for her? What if she had to accept me over and over again? What if one of those times... she didn't?

"Oh, look at this," Luke said, squatting to examine a set of paw prints.

"They're not that big," I said, secretly relieved that they were not the hoofprints I'd stumbled across before.

"Sure, all paw prints look small compared to yours," he said, squinting at them. "Thing is, they don't smell anything like a hellhound. I would guess it's just a dog."

"Pretty big for a dog," I said.

He shrugged and straightened, and we followed the scent.

Sure enough, it led us almost to the top of the bluff. It always felt almost heavenly up here, like we were standing in the sky and a tiny piece of Earth had just lifted up to touch our feet.

Scraggly pines clung to the rocky ground. After a moment, I noticed a low whining sound in the gaps of the breeze.

"Hey, buddy," Luke called out.

A silvery gray face peeked out from between two of the pines. It had long, floppy cheeks with webs of drool hanging from them.

"Great Dane," Luke said. "Come on, buddy, let's go find your owners."

The dog loped out from between the trees with quiet dignity. When it spotted me, it shied away slightly, probably recognizing something of the bear in me.

But Luke made a kissing sound and the big dog trotted right over to him, a silver tag on his collar catching the sunlight.

"I'll take this from here," Luke said. "You can head back to the castle if you want."

Surprisingly, that sounded very good. It wasn't like me to

prefer anything over being outdoors, but I felt like the bond was stretched thin and sharp as a wire between Cori and me. I had to get back to her.

"Thanks for the talk," I said gruffly and marched away before he could get sappy on me.

25

CORI

Soft morning light poured in the window of my lecture class. I kept glancing at the window, knowing Reed was out there with Luke, chasing down something dangerous.

I might be an overprotective maniac, but it upset me to think of Reed out there, vulnerable. Which I knew was crazy. What could they find that would be a match for the two of them? But my thoughts kept going back to those dark shapes in the water of the cave. And the bond between us kept buzzing and tightening. I felt like a kid whose socks slipped down into her boots. I could stand it, but the awareness of it took up about half my bandwidth.

All of a sudden, his overprotective nature made perfect sense.

"So today, we'll have a more in-depth talk about the price of magic," Professor Sora said in her soft voice. "This is a frightening concept, but important for us to talk about."

She began to pace across the front of the classroom. "Who here knows what the ultimate price means?"

I had no idea. I glanced around, but no one seemed to have any clue.

Then a girl in the front row raised her hand.

"Justine," Professor Sora said.

"The ultimate price is when a witch uses so much magic that her price is taken fully," Justine said softly.

"That is correct, dear," Professor Sora said, nodding. "The ultimate price is when a witch pushes her powers past her own limits, past her ability to pay."

The classroom was silent as we all took this in.

"When this happens, the witch pays her price permanently," Professor Sora said.

I blinked at her, the words jangling in my head until they nearly lost their meaning.

"The most famous example of the ultimate price is the story of Hattie's lover," Professor Sora said. "Hattie was a brilliant witch, such a gifted healer, that it was rumored she could prevent death itself."

Beside me, Bella leaned forward, intent, and I remembered that Bella had originally come to the school to learn how to heal her brother. I knew she was in a better place with the whole thing now, but she still had a keen interest in the healing arts. She said it called to her, which I thought was pretty cool.

"Hattie fell in love with an ordinary human," Professor Sora went on. "He was a simple man who worked on a farm by the lake, but he was kind. He played the lute and sang to her, and Hattie was happier than if she were being wooed by a king."

My fingers began drumming on my thighs. I could see where this was going.

"The price for Hattie's magic was great thirst," Professor Sora explained. "So she practiced her discipline to stave against it, of course. And she carried a skein of water with her everywhere, in case she had to call on her magic unprepared."

Thirst. That must be nice, I thought to myself.

"One day, she was walking in the village and the foreman from the farm where her lover worked ran up to her panting," Professor Sora continued. "Her lover had been horribly injured. She ran like the wind. But when she arrived, she knew it was too late."

Professor Sora strode over to the window and looked out for a moment, before turning to continue her story.

"Then she made her first mistake," she said, turning to us. "Hattie knew it was too late. But she decided to try anyway. She knelt by his side, blood soaking into her skirts. She placed her hands on his beautiful face, the only part of his body that wasn't injured."

Professor Sora paused dramatically for a moment, gazing over the classroom to be sure we were paying attention.

She didn't have to worry about that. You could have heard a pin drop.

"She closed her eyes and called on her magic," Professor Sora continued. "At first there was no effect. It was as if the magic had simply refused the impossible task. Then there was a stirring in the air, and Hattie's lover moaned in agony as his shattered bones tried to knit together."

Bella hissed in a breath beside me, and I tried to catch her eye to remind her it was an old story.

"Hattie worked on and on," Professor Sora said. "Her lover screamed and begged her to let him go, and her magic swirled out of her until only a fine mist remained. And then there was nothing, and still she raged on…"

Professor Sora stopped to push her spectacles up her

nose. "After a time, Hattie's lover died. And she wailed over his broken body. But no tears fell from her eyes. She searched her garments frantically for her skein, held it to her lips, and drank it dry."

I wasn't sure what was coming, but I was pretty sure I wasn't going to like it.

"She looked around in desperation, but there was no water near," the professor said. "So she dragged herself back toward the village as the foreman cried out her name. But she was so parched it was as if her body was turning inside out. And then she saw the cold lake, its surface dark and glossy."

The professor gazed out the window for a moment before turning back to us.

"They say the foreman jumped in after her and tried to pull her out, but her strength was superhuman. She drank in the cold water until the weight of it pulled her down. Most witches feel the drowning was a mercy."

She allowed a moment of silence, leaving us with the image of the torn body of the lover and Hattie's watery doom.

Bella put her hand up.

"Yes, Bella?" Professor Sora said.

"How do we know if a spell is too hard?" Bella asked softly.

Bella's price was losing colors from her vision, and once she lost her vision completely. But it came back to her quickly afterward. I could see that she was afraid of losing it permanently.

"So if we try a spell that's too hard, the price is forever?" Nuria asked, forgetting to raise her hand.

Other hands went up.

"Oh, my dears," Professor Sora said quickly. "This

doesn't happen by accident, so you've no need to worry. It doesn't come from and ordinary challenge. This is something that has to be done willfully."

"But how do you know if you're doing it?" Bella asked.

"Every witch has a limit," Professor Sora said. "A sort of wall at the end of her powers. You cannot push past it without knowing. The pain would be blindingly intense. You'd be more likely to accidentally climb the highest walls of the castle."

Hands went down, but there was still an air of tension in the room as a dozen new witches contemplated what our magic could mean if we pushed too far.

26

CORI

Later that afternoon, Reed and I headed into the woods.

He walked slightly ahead of me on the narrow trail, holding back branches with his big hands to give me easy passage and then scrambling through the foliage to get ahead of me again.

"Would you rather be a bear right now?" I asked as he jogged around me for about the hundredth time.

He paused and turned to me thoughtfully.

"Normally, yes," he said. "But these last few days, I just... feel good in this body."

I want to make you feel good in that body.

God, I was losing my mind.

"Are you okay with that?" he asked. "If you're tired, I can shift and carry you."

"No, I'm fine," I told him. "I was just curious. It seems like you like being a bear more than Luke likes being a wolf."

"Luke doesn't dislike being a wolf," he replied automatically.

"That wasn't what I meant," I said carefully. "I just mean... you were a bear in the tower. And when you chose me."

"I didn't really grow up in a human family," he said carefully.

"I'm sorry," I told him. "You were telling me the night we, uh, the night of the ceremony, that you came to live with the guardians when you were little?"

"Yes," he said.

We walked on in silence for a few minutes as I forced myself not to ask any follow-up questions. He would tell me what he wanted me to know. We had plenty of time to learn each other's secrets.

"It was a fire," he said at last. "My mother died in a fire."

"I'm so sorry, Reed," I told him over the sudden lump in my throat.

An image suddenly formed in my mind of a small version of him, all alone, dumped on the doorstep of a bunch of enormous guardians.

Hopefully, it hadn't been exactly like that.

"I didn't like them seeing me cry. It was... easier to be a bear at first," he said gruffly. "Everything is simpler for the bear. And old habits die hard."

"Reed, you don't ever have to be human with me if you don't want to," I told him honestly.

"We can't communicate when I'm a bear," he said softly.

"I'll bet we can," I told him. "It will just take practice."

He smiled at me and my heart almost stopped beating.

I wanted him so much. Tonight would be the night, I hoped. Tonight he would stake his claim. I guessed that was another thing we couldn't do when he was a bear. So maybe I did need him to be human for a while.

"We should keep going if we want to get there before full dark," he said gruffly.

"Sure," I said. "Of course."

We walked on quietly for a while.

By the time the trails ended, the cicadas had begun their nightsong. We were in the true forest now. I found myself stumbling over rocks and tree roots as the light slowly drained out of the woods.

Reed shot out a hand and caught me every time. I couldn't decide if it was romantic or spooky. Maybe it was both.

With the darkness came a notable drop in temperature. I cursed myself for only wearing my usual hooded sweatshirt. But I would be fine, as long as I didn't end up going for any more unplanned swims.

"I can shift and carry you," he reminded me. "It won't be easy from here on in."

"I'm okay," I lied, thinking about how surefooted, and warm, the bear would be. "But I'm glad for you to shift if you want."

His expression was torn.

"What's wrong?" I asked.

"I can protect you better as a bear," he said. "Does that seem chauvinistic?"

"Not even a little bit," I told him. "We're only walking, and I keep falling down. Imagine if I had to run from something."

"Yeah, that's what I keep doing," he said with a half-smile. "It's damned distracting."

I met his eyes and smiled at him as he sank and rose at the same time, every part of him changing except those beautiful golden eyes.

When he was fully in his other form, he lowered himself slightly, and I climbed on.

I felt more like a princess and less like a rodeo clown this time. Even when he picked up the pace and slammed through the foliage, I instinctively flattened myself with my face buried in his ruff and enjoyed the sensation of flying.

The forest blurred past in a sea of deepening green. I soaked in the warmth of the big bear and tried not to think about the fact that we were probably going someplace to climb a tree.

I wasn't a fan of caves, but I didn't particularly like heights either. Come to think of it, I wasn't really the outdoorsy type at all. But I was going to have to get used to it if I was hitching my wagon to a bear shifter. I could see myself growing to appreciate it more with the right company.

Without warning, the bear skidded to a stop. I had to squeeze my thighs around him to stop myself from flying forward.

We had come out at a clearing along the edge of a deep ravine. On the other side was a meadow with a tall tree at its center. Beyond that, the ground dropped away into another gorge, making the meadow seem almost like an island. This had to be home to the winter raven.

Reed began to lumber toward the ravine.

"Reed, what are you doing?" I asked, clinging to him desperately.

He kept moving.

"You know, you might have been able to jump across that thing on your own, but have you ever done it with a grown woman on your back?" I asked.

He didn't even slow down.

"I'm getting down," I said, letting go of his ruff. "You go on your own, if you're so anxious."

He turned his head back to me and I flung my right leg over and slid off him. He made a chuffing sound and looked around.

I wondered what the hell he could be looking for. Unless the Army Corps of Engineers was waiting around in these woods to build a bridge for us, we were going to have to find another way around this drop. It would take some time, but there was no way I was going to jump across.

After another moment of searching, Reed seemed to find what he was looking for. He lumbered over to a half-dead tree on the edge of the forest and nudged it with his nose.

"No way," I said.

But he wasn't listening to me. He grabbed the thing with his two front paws and heaved his weight against it. At first it only groaned. He shoved it twice more. On the third hit, a terrible crack split the air as the trunk snapped.

The tree seemed to fall across the ravine in slow motion, landing on the other side and bouncing twice before going still.

When I turned back to Reed, he was in his human form.

"Ready?" he asked, offering me his hand.

"You want us to walk across that thing?" I asked.

It seemed slightly less crazy than jumping, but only by a very small margin.

"Yes," he said. "Before it gets dark. Can I carry you?"

I narrowed my eyes at the fallen tree. The idea of walking on it was terrifying. But if I was going to be Reed's mate, I couldn't be the type of person who was afraid of a little physical challenge.

"I'm good," I said, taking his hand.

His eyebrows went up, but he didn't argue. He stepped onto the trunk just past the roots and I followed.

In my mind I had been hoping this might be kind of like that scene from my mom's favorite '80s movie, where the hot dance instructor takes the rich girl into the woods and makes her dance on a tree trunk over a creek.

In reality, it was terrifying.

Not one cell of me wanted to giggle or flirt, or do the mambo. Branches were sticking out all over the place. Insects and birds were fleeing for their lives. The tree wasn't a bridge, it was a cadaver, or maybe a fallen planet.

Reed's hand tightened around mine and I could tell he felt my fear through the bond.

But I was too scared to be ashamed. I clung to him in the gathering darkness and swore to myself I would not look down, not even when a thick branch snapped off under my foot and fell into the gorge. I paused for a moment, waiting for the sound of it as it hit the bottom, but it never came.

We're really high up.

We pushed on, the trunk growing narrower and sporting more dead branches as we got deeper into the leafless canopy and closer to the other side.

It didn't seem possible that it would continue to support us the whole way. I had to trust Reed's instincts. He moved slowly and carefully, but without hesitation.

The trunk was bouncing under our feet now. Branches caught at my skirts with every step, and I had to stop and untangle myself.

"Almost there," he murmured. "I'm going to jump off, and you're going to jump too."

"No," I moaned.

But he was right, that was the fastest way to get ourselves

off this tree. And it was better than putting our weight on the smallest branches.

He counted to three, and when he leapt from the tree I did too.

He landed hard on the grassy meadow on the other side, falling into a roll and pulling me on top of him. We lay on the ground panting in a messy tangle of limbs.

Then Reed began to laugh.

The sound was deep and rusty and magnificent.

I began to laugh too, in spite of myself.

"You know I could have jumped across that gorge in like two seconds, right?" he asked me, his golden eyes dancing. "Even with you on my back."

"But then I would have missed an opportunity to see you knock over an innocent tree," I teased.

"It was dead already," he said defensively.

"I know," I told him.

Suddenly, the heated lightning was back between us, pulling me into his orbit. The meadow was fading, the darkening sky above didn't matter anymore. There was only Reed and those beautiful golden eyes...

"Look," he whispered, tilting his chin upward.

I dragged my eyes from his to search the sky, where a snow-white raven circled above us.

27

REED

Cori's face lit up as she saw the white raven. This was more than just relief that we had found the bird, she was in awe of its beauty.

And I was in awe of hers. It was clear she wasn't much of a hiker, but she had been a trooper today. I loved the way she looked in the last rays of daylight, after a march through the woods, with grass stains on her gown and just a few leaves in her dark curls of her hair. Like she could be the mate of a half-feral, man-bear like me.

"Keep your eye on her," I whispered. "We need to pay attention to where she goes."

Cori nodded without taking her eyes off the bird, her curls bouncing in a merry way. We watched in breathless silence as the raven swirled in the sky and then alighted on a low branch of the big tree.

"That was easy," Cori whispered back excitedly.

"So far," I agreed, tasting the air. "Trouble is, we're upwind of her now. If we get too close, we'll spook her. We need to get around to the other side of the tree without her noticing us. Once we do, we'll have to figure out how to get close enough to get a feather."

"I know a sleeping spell," Cori said thoughtfully. "If we're close enough, it may work. She'll sleep for a few minutes, just long enough for us to get what we need."

"Perfect," I told her, trying not to worry about the price of her magic. "Let's go. But slowly."

We got carefully to our feet. I noticed how Cori was even trying to keep her skirts from rustling.

She wasn't a woodsman. She would be about as subtle out here as an air horn, compared to any one of my brothers. But she was trying, and I loved her for it.

Given enough time, I could teach her the forest skills she needed. I was sure of it.

We picked our way around the edges of the meadow. I glanced up every few steps, but the raven remained on her perch.

At last, we reached the other side of the tree.

Cori met my eyes, questioning without speaking.

I nodded to her. This was the perfect time to do her spell.

She closed her eyes, just as she had in the cave last night. I could feel her releasing her hold on the world.

I had felt a little of the flavor of this before, but our continued time together must have strengthened our bond. I wasn't getting the exact details of her thoughts, but I could taste the desire to cleanse her mind and settle it.

She lifted and released her consciousness, like it was a hot air balloon drifting over a meadow. I could feel the energy ripple the air near her.

When she opened her eyes again, her lips were moving, palms uplifted. But there was no glowing ball like the light she'd formed in the cave.

My eyes went to the winter raven and I saw that she was sitting very still on the edge of her nest.

"That will make her nice and sleepy for now," Cori whispered.

I was relieved to see that Cori wasn't confused or frightened of me.

"You feel okay?" I asked her.

"Fine," she said. "I paid in advance with the meditation I just did. Plus I did some prep work this morning."

"That's good," I told her, feeling relieved.

We approached the tree carefully as the bird remained perfectly still. We had nearly reached her when something whistled through the air from behind us. Its acrid scent invaded my senses before I saw it, and I cringed a little at the smell.

A flaming arrow, glowing with some kind of strange magic cut the darkness between Cori and me.

There was a horrible ruffling, thwacking sound and the winter raven exploded into a mist of shimmering ashes right before our eyes.

Cori cried out in surprise.

I turned to see who had fired the arrow. It would have been an incredible shot for a regular arrow, but this one was obviously enchanted, which probably helped it find its mark.

Behind us, across the other side of the gorge, a man sat on an enormous horse, watching us.

But it was no ordinary horse. It's mane and fetlocks were made of flame that flickered menacingly, as if they might leap free and spread to the nearby trees at any moment.

Instinctively, I stopped between the archer and my mate, eyeing the distance and lining up the jump that would take me to him. But the gorge was too wide on that side. There was no way I would make it, as a human or a bear.

And the longer I looked at that fiery horse, the less sure I became.

Focus, Reed, I told myself. If he was going to get away, which seemed likely if the wicked horse was as fast as it looked, then I had to note all the details. I couldn't let my fear of fire overwhelm me.

I focused on the man. He had pale skin, but wore a black mask and a dark hood that hid his features. A feathery bundle, that could only be the winter raven's mate was tied to his pack.

He was clearly a member of the Order of the Broken Blade, and he wasn't even bothering to hide it. Luke was right - they were getting bold. This one had been willing to reveal himself in broad daylight, and willing to kill the female raven in order to stop us. And because he already had the other bird, they had all the feathers they needed for their spell.

The horse stomped its feet and the scent carried cleanly to me, sending a shiver of horror down my spine. It was midnight black, tall and broad like a draft horse, but its mane and tail were alive with flames. There was no mistaking that it was the source of the magical flames that had burned down the old tree.

And it had taken a bevy of trained witches to put that out.

The man spoke to the beast and it half-reared onto its thick back legs before they galloped away, the horse's flaming tail billowing out behind it.

Fear closed around my heart like a frozen fist, and I dragged in a shuddering breath.

28

CORI

I watched Reed stare after the magical horse and archer as the last rays of sunlight faded, leaving us alone in the darkness.

His fear was palpable, and my own heart clenched in sympathy. He had said his mother died in a fire. The horse must have brought up buried fears.

"So no feather then," I said softly, hoping to distract him from the haunting pain.

He turned to me, his face soft with some emotion that I couldn't describe, flames dancing in his golden eyes as if they were still reflecting back the sight of that nightmarish horse.

"We can try to find her nest," he said, blinking and running a hand through his tangled hair. "There could be a feather in there."

"Where would that be?" I asked encouragingly.

He glanced up at the tree we were standing under.

"No way," I breathed, looking up into the mighty canopy towering over us.

"I see them in this meadow a lot," he told me. "It makes sense that they would nest in the tree."

I nodded, afraid to reply. The forest had been tough, but not terrible. But I wasn't the kind of person who would climb a tree even under ideal circumstances.

And this was pretty far from ideal. I was wearing a school gown and it was full dark out, with nothing but the moon to light the hulking giant of a tree.

"I'm a good climber in bear form," he told me. "But I can't do delicate work."

"What do you mean?" I asked.

"I can climb up there, but if there's a feather in the nest, I won't be able to pluck it out," he said.

"I want to be a team player, but I can't climb that tree," I told him bluntly.

He made a small coughing sound that I sincerely hoped wasn't covering a snicker.

"I have a different plan," he said. "I'll shift and you ride on my back. When we get up there, you'll look for the feather."

I gulped.

"It'll be like a piggyback ride," he said.

"What if I start to fall off," I worried, thinking about that glossy fur and the distance between the ground and the top of that towering tree.

"Cori Silverman, I will not let you fall," he told me.

Warmth spread in my chest, as if I had just bolted down half a cup of hot tea. He was telling the truth.

"Okay," I said. "I can't believe we're doing this, but okay."

"Good girl," he said with a pirate's grin.

I watched as he sank into bear form, thinking it would seem less magical this time, since I had already seen it tonight.

But was just as unbelievable. I wasn't sure I'd ever get used to it.

He approached me, thrusting his forehead down like he knew I was going to pat it.

He was totally right. I did want to pat him. We greeted each other for a moment, me running my fingers through that velvety pelt and him snuffling and snorting with pleasure.

Then he lowered himself down.

I hesitated this time. Letting him carry me up that tree was beyond a trust exercise. We could both die.

But when he lifted his chin to urge me onto his back I obeyed. My instinct to follow his lead already ran too deep.

This time when I slipped onto his back, he waited for me to have a good hold, and then slowly stood up on his hind paws. I had to wrap my thighs around him harder than usual and lock my arms around his neck to stay on, but it felt about as secure as it could.

He approached the tree and pulled himself up, as if knowing that just holding on this way would be an effort for me.

I closed my eyes and buried my face in his fur. I didn't like feeling the effort he made to find a good branch, or the knowledge that the ground was disappearing beneath us.

He climbed on and on. My arms were getting tired just from holding on, but there was no danger that I would let go. I was too terrified for that.

Suddenly, his movement stopped.

I opened my eyes, hoping we'd reached our goal. But there was no nest in sight.

The bear was gazing up to the thinner branches above.

A big, circular bundle of sticks rested on one of them.

"The nest," I breathed.

But he didn't move.

It took me a second to figure out the problem. He couldn't go up any further. The branches would break under us.

Only one of us light enough to get up there.

Me.

"No," I whispered.

But I already knew I would do it. I had seen that guy shoot the winter raven out of the air like it was nothing. I couldn't let the Order of the Broken Blade threaten my friends, or my mate.

"Fine," I whispered. "Stay under me, though. We both know I might fall."

And though he couldn't answer in words, I felt that same wash of warmth in my chest.

Cori Silverman, I will not let you fall.

It didn't seem like it should be enough, but it was.

I managed to unlock my arms and grab onto the nearest branch.

29

CORI

My hands were shaking as I moved slowly from branch to thinning branch.

I knew Reed was below me waiting, ready to snatch me out of the air if I fell. But I couldn't so much as glance down at him to be sure.

If I looked down at the ground, I knew I'd be petrified and freeze in place - too low to reach the nest and too high for Reed to reach me. We might be hanging out in this tree for the better part of a week before anyone found us.

So I kept my eyes on the nest above, and willed my heart not to beat through my chest.

The next branch I grabbed bent instantly, and I had to try a few before finding one that would support me.

All those meditations we had learned in class helped me to focus my mind on the task at hand, finding the next good branch and then the next one after that, staying close to the trunk for as long as I could.

By some miracle, or more likely by design, the ravens had built their sturdy nest in a crook between two of the larger branches in the canopy. When I reached it at last, I was able to crawl out slightly from the trunk.

My hands were sticky with sap. At least if I found a feather my shaking hands wouldn't be able to drop it.

I belly crawled onto the lower limb and peered up into the nest.

It was a lovely thing, with rough sticks on the outside and soft moss on the inside. I could see some downy little tufts on the edges of the nest, but no real feathers - nothing you could turn into a quill.

To see any deeper inside, I would have to move closer and lift myself up off the branch.

The temptation to climb back down was almost overwhelming, but I had come this far.

In for a penny...

I held my breath as I eased my weight outward and pushed up.

The branch beneath me bent, but didn't break. And the nest was lowered with that movement, so that suddenly instead of just seeing the edges, I could see the whole nest.

There were still no large feathers inside, much to my dismay.

But the nest wasn't empty.

Two tiny, downy creatures sat in the center. They cheeped at me plaintively, their yellow beaks lifted high.

I gazed down at them, my heart broken as I realized that both their parents, possibly the only winter ravens in the world, were gone, and never coming back.

I knew nothing about raising hatchlings, but I couldn't leave them here.

The nest was too big to carry, but maybe I could scoop the little ones up in my hand. Though there was no way I was getting back down to Reed one-handed.

I made the mistake of glancing down at him and felt immediately dizzy. The bear was far enough below to look small.

Breathe, Cori, breathe...

The chicks were still crying. I had to do something.

I eased myself back down onto the branch and pulled off my hooded cloak, then eased it back on backwards, so that the hood was in the front, like a bib.

When I raised myself up again, the babies began chirping at me. I took a deep breath and then scooped them up in my right hand.

They were so tiny they were almost weightless.

I lowered them into the hood of my cloak. They were cuddled together, but they didn't look too unhappy. Hopefully, it would be warm and homey enough to get them back to the castle where someone could tell me what to do next.

The idea of going back down was much more frightening than climbing up had been. But I had no choice. I scooted backward on the branch, back toward the trunk.

"Don't worry, little ones," I crooned. "We just have to get to Reed, and he'll get us all home okay."

Reed gave a groan, as if to ask what I had said.

"Nothing," I called to him. "There were babies in the nest. I'm bringing them with us."

He groaned again, this time it had a complaining tone, but I was too busy trying to find a foothold to worry about it.

The descent seemed to take forever. I measured my progress branch by branch, taking care not to crush the chicks against my chest or the tree.

Suddenly something big and warm nudged my ankle. I fought back a scream, then realized it was Reed.

He made a low growling-chuffing sound of greeting that

somehow made me think of cozy sweaters and nights by the fire.

I relaxed instantly and allowed him to slide his back under me.

"I can't hold on as tightly this time," I told him. "I don't want to crush the babies."

He turned his head to snuffle my chest.

The little birds cheeped at him, and he withdrew his snout indignantly.

I held back my surprised giggle.

"See," I told him. "They need our help. Just get us back to the castle, and we'll figure out what to do."

He began to lumber down the tree as I held tight to his ruff. I hoped my iron grip didn't hurt him, but he honestly didn't seem to notice.

Finally, we reached the ground.

"Oh, thank God," I said, sliding off his back and stretching my legs.

He looked on while I shook out the tension of the climb. Then instead of shifting back, he lowered himself again, as if urging me to climb back on.

"You don't have to carry me," I hedged. He must be tired too. Though I would have loved to ride...

He stayed down and eyed me intently.

"Okay, thank you," I told him earnestly.

He held still while I climbed on, and then we walked across the meadow, back toward the ravine.

This time, he didn't hesitate. He just took three big strides and launched us into the air. By the time I could even think to be worried, we were already safely on the other side.

The bear made a sound that was about as close to *I told*

you so as a bear could make, and then we walked into the darkened forest, back toward the castle.

30
CORI

I didn't have a watch, but it was clearly very late by the time we reached the castle. The windows were dark, and the moonlight was the only thing showing us the way home. I suspected we were in that gray area that could either be really late, or really early, depending on what side of it you were on.

Reed shifted back into his human form as we made our way through the boxwood labyrinth. As we stepped into the courtyard, we spotted a dark figure heading for the rear door of the castle.

"Hello," Reed practically growled as stepped protectively in front of me.

"Oh," said a surprised and familiar female voice.

"Kendall?" I asked.

"Hello, Cori," she mumbled, looking pretty bummed out.

"Are you okay?" I asked her.

"I'm fine," she replied. "I was... going to meet someone in town, but he never showed."

I was impressed that she'd been honest. Kendall was normally the epitome of cool as a cucumber.

If I thought she was going to stick around for sympathy though, I was wrong. She turned on her heel began to march away. But before she got more than a few steps away, the wind picked up and the baby birds began chirping pitifully.

"What was that?" she asked, turning back and narrowing her eyes suspiciously.

"We found some baby birds," I told her.

She came back to look. "What are you going to do with them?"

"I have no idea," I admitted. "And it's too late to wake up Professor Waita."

"They're super cute," she said. "Maybe Anya can help you. She's really good with animals."

"I'll ask her in the morning," I told her, as Reed held open the door to the castle for us.

We went silent when we entered. I wasn't really sure if I could get in trouble for being out late, since I was technically supposed to be with my intended mate. But Kendall definitely wasn't supposed to be wandering the hallways.

When we reached the top of the center stairs, she turned off toward her room and Reed and I continued toward the tower.

Either the chicks had fallen asleep, or they were respecting the implied rule of silence. I was just grateful that they weren't announcing us. The last thing I wanted to do was wake anyone up.

My classmates might love to have some juicy gossip about me sneaking around at night with Reed instead of... accepting the bond. But I liked to keep my private life private.

It occurred to me that our time might actually be running out to seal the bond. We'd spent that first night putting out the fire, so there hadn't been any real time for anything else. And then last night there had definitely been something else. I tried not to think about the way he'd touched me in the bath, for fear I would lose myself down that road and just throw myself at him in the stairwell.

I wasn't sure if that first night counted or not, since the deal was three nights in his bed. But if it did, then tonight was night three, and it was quickly slipping away from us.

I made a mental note to ask him about it, as soon as we were far away from the sleeping witches of Primrose Academy.

"Come," Reed whispered when we reached the tower door.

I turned to him and he scooped me up in his arms. Before I could argue, he was flying up the stairs with me, a wicked grin on his face.

"H-holy crap," I said, when he set me on my feet in his room.

"You thought bears were slow and bumbling, didn't you?" he teased.

"But you're not *in* bear form," I said. "And you're not even out of breath."

"It's just one of the perks of being a shifter," he said.

The corners of his beautiful mouth were ever so slightly upturned. He liked the compliment, even if he was shrugging it off.

I wondered vaguely how someone like Reed could ever be starved for compliments. He was strong, smart and wildly gorgeous.

"What are you thinking about?" he asked.

"Wondering what we can do for the babies," I lied, looking down at the little creatures in my hood.

"Maybe we can make them some sort of nest," he suggested.

"I wonder what we can feed them," I said. "Do you think they'll make it all night without food?"

"They would be asleep in the wild," he assured me. "Let's see what would make a good nest."

We rummaged around his kitchen and found a mixing bowl that was only a little smaller than the nest where we'd found the babes.

Reed curled two of his t-shirts up and covered the bottom of the bowl with them, then spread another across the top to create a smooth surface.

"Do you think that's okay?" he asked.

"It was just sticks and moss outside," I said, shrugging. "It looks cozy to me."

He watched as I carefully scooped the babies out of my hood and placed them onto the t-shirts. They cheeped sadly, like they didn't want to be woken up.

"You're okay, little ones," I cooed.

After a moment they snuggled close and went promptly back to sleep, each one resting its head on the other's downy body.

"We did it," Reed said softly, looking down at the tiny birds.

I sighed and felt the fear and adrenaline slowly draining out of me, so that I realized I was bone tired.

"What a night," I said softly.

"You were so brave," he told me, his golden eyes solemn.

Suddenly, I wasn't so sleepy anymore. Electricity danced between us, waking every cell in my body.

Reed reached out and caressed my cheek with the rough pad of his thumb.

I closed my eyes and leaned into his touch.

"Cori," he murmured against my lips.

I was melting, my whole body a sea of want.

Suddenly, he tensed and pulled away.

"Someone's coming," he growled, stalking toward the door.

I froze, watching him, and wondering who in the world would be on the tower stairs at this hour.

"It's your friend," he said after a moment, with a slight smile.

"Which friend?" I asked.

"The strange little one," he replied as someone knocked.

He opened the door to reveal Anya waiting on the other side.

"Hey," she said sheepishly. "Is Cori here?"

He gestured to where I stood by the counter with the bowl full of baby birds.

"Kendall told me you needed help with some baby birds," Anya said, marching over and eyeing the metal mixing bowl suspiciously. "You have them in there?"

"It's not what it looks like," I said. "We put t-shirts in there to make it warmer."

"Well, I'm glad you're not tossing them with some blue cheese and tomatoes," she teased, taking a look at the babies. "They're super cute. You did a great job with the shirts making it soft. But we need disposable bedding. Can you shred some fabric or paper that we can put under them for now?"

"Sure," I said. "Reed can you sacrifice one more shirt? And do you have some scissors?"

"On it," he said, disappearing into the alcove.

"He seems more… domesticated than last time I saw him," Anya whispered to me.

"Weirdly, he was pretty domesticated from the beginning. When he's in human form at least," I said. "He just likes being a bear."

"I feel that," Anya said, nodding.

I smiled at the idea. Anya was so petite and delicate. I couldn't picture her as a bear at all. Though maybe that was why she understood *wanting* to be a bear. I had always hated taking up so much space. But maybe if I were small and slender, I'd want to have a bigger presence.

Reed came back in and sat on his mattress with a couple of shirts.

Before I could ask if he needed scissors, he was tearing the thing to shreds with his bare hands.

"That's a handy skill," Anya said.

We watched him for a moment.

"Did Kendall wake you up?" I asked her.

"Not on purpose," she replied. "But our room isn't that big. And I think she was upset. She got stood up tonight by the guy she's seeing."

"Yeah, it sucks," I said. "Have you met him?"

"As far as I know, no one has," she told me quietly. "But up until now she seemed really happy about him. Hopefully, it was just a miscommunication or something."

"I'm sure that's it," I said.

"Well, I guess I should let you guys get some rest," Anya said. "Do you want me to take the birds for tonight?"

"Oh my gosh, do you want to?" I asked, feeling super relieved.

"Yes, of course," she said. "I love animals and these guys are amazing."

I turned to see how Reed had made out with the bird bedding.

The big bear shifter was fast asleep, a pile of shredded t-shirts by his side.

"Oh wow, you wore him out," Anya said.

"Not the way you think," I told her. "We were trying to get a feather from the winter raven to make the quill. But one of the Order got there first - stole one raven and killed the other. That's why we had to take the babies. It was awful. I don't know what we're going to do."

"Hey," Anya said, placing her hand on my arm. "We'll figure it out. Look on the bright side. You saved the babies, and you didn't get yourselves killed."

"You're a really good friend, you know that?" I asked her.

She beamed at me.

I slipped over to the mattress and grabbed the shredded shirts.

Anya was already cradling the bowl in her arms, so I tucked the shreds into her pocket for her.

"See you in a bit," she whispered as she slipped out.

It was only when the door closed behind her that I realized the pink light of dawn was already bleeding in the windows.

I crawled into bed next to Reed. It couldn't hurt to get a few minutes of sleep before class.

He curled protectively around me without waking, and in spite of all our adventures and my worries, I felt myself drifting off to sleep almost immediately in the warmth of his arms.

31

CORI

Warm sunlight dappled the work stations in Professor Waita's classroom, and I found my thoughts drifting back to Reed, as they had all day.

Waking up in his arms had been incredible. Wrenching myself out of them to run to classes hadn't. We had slept through breakfast, so now my stomach was grumbling and I was feeling cranky from getting so little sleep.

But thinking about Reed lifted my spirits every time. And while we hadn't sealed the bond last night, it felt like the adventure we'd had together was just as important. We had worked together, faced defeat and kept going.

I asked him about whether the first night counted or not, and he said he wasn't sure, but it was probably best if we didn't let a fourth night pass, just to be safe. It might be harder to seal the bond after that. Not that it wouldn't be fun to try.

"Today we're doing a practical, ladies," Professor Waita said with a smile.

I repressed a sigh. It was usually a practical magic lab in Plants class, but I had hoped I might get lucky and we'd have an advanced demonstration instead, so I could just relax and take notes.

"We're going to work on crossing plants," the professor said, her warm brown face a study in delight. "This is more complicated than some of our other lessons, but I'm excited to see each of you use your creativity to bring a new idea to life."

She began rolling around a cart with two boxes of flowering plants in it. One set of plants had red blossoms, the other had white. She placed one of each color in front of every student as she spoke.

"I'd like you to combine the two plants, using a joining spell," she said. "What you combine it into is completely up to you. But by the end of class I'd like to see that each of you has a successful hybrid."

In the row in front of me, Esme was already moving her hands and murmuring over her plants. It wasn't fair that some people were beautiful, popular, *and* talented.

She caught me looking and gave me a smirk.

Definitely unfair when those people were also mean.

The professor placed my plants in front of me and gave me a gentle smile.

"Relax, Cori," she said quietly. "You've got this."

Gratitude made tears prickle my eyes, but she was already moving on to the next row, her gray and brown bun bobbing as she looked up and down from cart to student.

I stared down at my plants and wondered if they were capable of making decisions. If they were, I hoped they would decide to work with me.

"Let's begin," Professor Waita said, depositing the now-empty cart beside her podium.

I took a deep breath and closed my eyes, pulling my energy in close and tight like a ball, and then letting it expand out across my chest, my table, the whole room, and then in again.

When I opened my eyes again, a quaver of sparkling energy hovered over my palms.

I traced it over the plants, whispering a joining spell that I hoped would cause each plant to have both red and white blossoms. It wasn't especially impressive, but it seemed like something I could pull off.

In the row in front of me, Dozie had blended the colors of her flowers into a perfectly balanced pink.

I tried to focus on my own work, but it was hard to concentrate over the squeals of happiness in the front row. Esme had turned all of her flowers into red and white checkerboards.

I glanced over at Kendall. Her flowers had alternating red and white petals now. She caught me looking and shrugged.

Focus, Cori.

I gathered myself again, closing my eyes, pulling in my energy and letting it breathe out into my palms. This time when I opened my eyes, I kept them on my own work.

I traced my hands over the flowers, pulling the energy over them. I could feel them awakening. Their inner voices were high and sweet, a gentle whisper of life.

I murmured back to them, telling them what I had in mind.

They went still and quiet. I was just starting to think that maybe the spell had fizzled completely when there was flurry of movement.

Multiple tiny blossoms began to unfurl on each plant. The red blossoms were on the red plant and the white on the white, but I hadn't killed the plants or blown anything up. This was as close as I was going to get to a victory.

I looked over at Kendall to see if she had noticed my triumph, but she was gazing down at my plants with an expression of horror.

A hissing sound came from my table and I looked back to find an unfolding scene of chaos. The tiny red and white flowers were battling each other, stems bending, leaves smacking, until petals rained into their pots.

I bent down to whisper for them to stop, but one of the red flowers gave out a high-pitched roar and a white blossom snapped at me, petals clamping down way too close to my nose.

"Oh my," Professor Waita said, heading over to take a look.

The red plant was definitely winning now. White petals snowed down on my workstation.

"Please, stop," I whispered. But the magic was long gone from my hands. I would have to start over.

"Well, I've certainly never seen anything like this before," the professor said thoughtfully. "Congratulations."

She walked on before I could figure out whether or not she was being sarcastic.

On my table, the white plant was dead, and the red was withering. Without a common enemy, the red blossoms had turned on each other. It was only a matter of time until both plants were no more.

No matter how powerful or unusual my magic was, there was one undeniable thread running through it.

Everything my magic touched was ruined.

Whether I was knocking statues into my classmates, sealing up icy chambers, or making plants murder each other, my magic was chaos.

Leaving school to go with Reed might be the smartest thing I could ever do. All he needed from me was love, and the ability to be a mother to his children.

For an instant I let the classroom fade away so I could picture it.

We were in a sweet cottage in the woods, like Luke and Bella's. A fire crackled in the grate, and something sweet was baking in the kitchen. Reed sat in his chair, as I rocked a baby in my arms. The child had his father's golden eyes and my dark curly hair. My heart throbbed at the sight of him, even though I knew I had only dreamed him up myself. He wasn't real.

But he could be. I wasn't perfect, but this was something I could do.

A shifter needed a witch to have a shifter child. Without her magic, it would be impossible. My life would have purpose.

And then the truth hit me.

The notebook and pen fell from my hand and clattered on the classroom floor.

"Cori," Kendall said. "Cori, are you okay?"

I lowered myself into my seat, head in my hands, unable to speak, even to my friend.

How could I not have seen it before?

Reed was relying on my magic to produce a shifter child. But my magic ruined everything it touched. I couldn't risk that.

My chaotic powers would only endanger a child. If I could have one at all. And if I couldn't, then what good was I to him?

There was no way I could really be with Reed.

He would have to choose another, competent witch for his mate.

I pulled myself out of my chair and ran from the room.

32

REED

The day passed slowly as I waited to see Cori again. Adventuring all evening and then sleeping right through what remained of our night had left me feeling hollow and hungry.

Especially since last night was intended to be our last, according to the old ways. I had to claim her before another night passed, or set her free.

The madness of it had me spiraling, and I had spent most of the morning and afternoon patrolling in bear form trying to distract myself from my thoughts.

The bear was less anxious and more furious. His feelings were uncomplicated. He liked the girl, he wanted the girl, he would have the girl.

By the time the sun began to fade, and I rose back into my regular form, he had me thinking along the same lines and feeling a low rumble of confidence at my ability to keep the little witch safe and happy.

After all, her magic was her own, whether she was with me or not. Arguably she would be less likely to find herself under threat with a shifter guardian mate and strapping young sons to protect her.

The price for her magic was horrible. But it was her price, with or without me.

And the truth of the matter was, my own price for being without her was too dear to imagine. I had barely made it through the day. If she lost her memories sometimes or got confused, I would help her. That was what you did when you loved someone.

And I loved Cori. She held my battered heart in her small, sweet hands.

I strode back toward the school, feeling ready to face whatever our futures held. It was just about time for the final classes of the day to let out.

Before I made it to the doors, they flew open and Cori's whole group of friends came pouring out into the courtyard.

"Reed," Cori called to me, then got a funny look on her face.

Actually, her face looked different, puffy somehow, and her eyes were wet with tears.

"Are you okay?" I asked her. Fury rose in my chest at whatever had made her feel this way.

"We have news," the one with the purple glasses said.

"What kind of news?" I asked.

"Good news and bad news," she replied, pushing the glasses up her nose. "Nina and I finished translating the other details about the spell."

I looked to Nina. Her pretty brown face was a picture of concern.

"What's wrong?" I asked her as gently as I could.

"It's the timing," she said. "According to the references to the planetary alignments, the ceremony has to be done tonight for the best chance of success."

"So the Order will be doing it tonight," I breathed.

"And that means so are we," Nina said.

"We can't," I told her, thinking of Cori. There was no way I could let another night pass without claiming her and sealing our bond.

"We don't have a choice," Cori said, looking down at her hands.

I wanted to grab her by the shoulders and scream at her to tell me what was wrong. But I remembered how she felt the last time I yelled at her in front of her friends.

"We don't have all the items on the list," I remembered.

"We do have some good news about that," Nina said with a smile.

Just then, the doors from the castle burst open again and Anya appeared in the frame, two big white birds on her shoulders.

"Look at them," she crowed proudly. "Just look."

We all watched as she marched over with a beautiful winter raven on each shoulder, a look of maternal pride on her face.

"How did you do that?" I asked.

"She used the growing spell we learned in our plants class last month," Lark said. "With some variations, of course."

"And they were very receptive to magic," Anya said fondly, touching her nose to the beak of the raven on her right shoulder. "Meet Calvin and Hobbes."

"The pleasure is mine," I said.

The birds eyed me suspiciously, but didn't fly off, so I considered it a win.

"Luke was tracking the Order as soon as we found out about the timing," Lark went on. "He said they're setting up for the ceremony on the north side of the valley, which means we need to do our counter spell on the south side of the bluff."

"I'm not really a magic guy," I admitted.

"Nina and I are going to go make the ink for the spell," Lark said. "Anya is going to convince one of the ravens to give her a feather she can form into a quill."

"Okay," I said, eyeing Cori, who still wasn't looking at me.

"We were hoping that you and Cori could go prep the site on the bluff," Lark said.

"I can help Anya," Cori said immediately.

"Oh no, I'm fine," Anya said. "Go with Reed."

Cori buttoned her lip and nodded.

My chest felt like it was caving in. She didn't want to be with me. She didn't want me to claim her. I felt like the Earth was dissolving and there was nothing I could do.

"Ready?" I asked her.

At least we would be alone when she told me.

She nodded miserably and we headed off into the night.

33

REED

I expected that she would start talking during the hike up to the bluff, but I was wrong.

We walked through the courtyard, traversed the maze, and trampled through the darkening forest in silence.

I tried to tell myself that the hike was harder for her than for me. But even when we got to the place where the trees thinned, she still said nothing.

The space between us seemed to pulse and bristle with emotion. I couldn't reach through it to touch her, even though I wanted to more than anything.

Surely, she would talk to me when we reached our destination.

We came out on the bluff to the jaw-dropping sight of the valley spread out before us. The wind blew cold and sweet here, carrying the scent of the pines and the cool, clear water of the river below.

"We need to clear the space for the circle," Cori said. Her voice sounded small in the wind.

"How big of a space do we need?" I asked her.

"I'll pace it out," she offered.

She moved slowly, carefully, and I almost smiled at the serious expression on her face.

When the bounds of the circle were marked, we began clearing out the rocks and sticks. We moved quickly, never touching, never speaking, until nothing extraneous remained inside the circle.

Cori pulled sage and a lighter from her cloak and set the sage alight.

I clenched my jaw, but managed not to flinch away from her.

"Oh," she said suddenly. "I'm sorry, Reed. I forgot."

"I was only a child," I said, feeling defensive. "It stuck with me, that's all. I'm usually fine, but sometimes it sneaks up on me."

"It's okay," she said, fixing me with those lovely, solemn eyes. "Fire is dangerous."

"Cori," I said helplessly, unable to take it anymore. "I don't know what I did wrong, but please let me make it right."

"You didn't do anything wrong," she said, turning away, but not before I could see her expression close off again.

"I want to be your mate," I told her, throwing caution to the wind. "I love you and I want to care for you. I long for you. And I want to love and protect you, and our children, too."

She didn't reply, just stood there, frozen.

"But I want you to have what you want, too," I went on. "Do you want to stay at school? Do you want to start a family now? Do you just want to be with me? How can I make you happy?"

"You can't," she sobbed.

The two words were like a dagger through my heart.

I stood there, reeling as she ran from me.

As the wind howled, and the sound of my mate's footsteps disappeared, I wondered how my heart would continue to beat.

34

CORI

Tree branches seemed to be reaching out to stop me, roots tangling out of the soil to slow my path.

But I was too heartbroken to care that my gown was ripped, and my shoes were sodden.

Reed loved me.

His words were still ringing in my ears - all the words I'd longed to hear him say.

He wanted me, he longed for me. He wanted us to have a family.

It had been so long since I had felt like part of something - like I belonged. Even the school didn't want me.

Reed was offering me everything I had ever dreamed of - love acceptance, and my own choices.

And I had to walk away.

None of it changed the realization I'd had in plants class today. My magic was destructive, and I couldn't let anyone else rely on it. Not Reed - not the children he so desperately wanted - not even me. I wasn't a good enough witch to be a student. Loving me was dangerous for Reed.

And I cared for him too much to put him in danger. And

I could never risk having the life of a child rely on my disastrous magic.

The tears I'd been fighting off all day burned in my eyes, and I let them fall freely. There was no one here to see it.

I was Cori Silverman, and I would always be alone.

When the tears finally slowed, I gasped for breath and leaned back against a tree to think.

I couldn't be with Reed. And the school didn't want me.

I had spent all day trying to figure out what I was supposed to do next. But the answer was clear to me now.

I would help my friends, because that was what friends did.

But tonight, when it was all over, I would pack up my things and head home. My parents might have a boring life, but it was theirs, and I was their daughter.

I didn't need to have shifters or magic in my world. If I could tamp down my emotions, I could probably hide my magic for the rest of my life.

It sounded awful, but less awful than inadvertently hurting the people I loved. Especially when one of those people was Reed.

I wiped the tears from my face, took a deep breath, and resolved to march right back up to the bluff and tell Reed my plan.

35

REED

By the time Cori returned, her friends were already gathering on the bluff. They didn't ask me where she was, but I think it was only because they felt sorry for me.

The young witches tiptoed around, arranging things, and chatting nervously about Bella and Luke's journey down to the valley to observe the other ceremony.

If we were here, performing a counter spell and it didn't work, at least Bella and Luke would be close at hand to the other ceremony, along with the rest of the Brotherhood of Guardians. Maybe they could disrupt it in a more physical way.

My heart ached for Luke. I knew how hard it was for me to see the woman I loved in danger. I couldn't imagine how he must feel, bringing his bonded mate closer to the enemies.

As soon as I had stopped thinking about my own pain for a moment, Cori's sweet scent carried to me across the windy bluff.

I turned to see her trooping out of the woods, back

toward the circle. She had obviously been crying. But now she wore an expression of naked determination.

She didn't want me. It was clear.

I marched over to her, heartsick, but eager to do her one last kindness. I loved her. Her happiness was more important to me than my own.

"Cori," I said.

Her eyes were so sad.

"Let's talk privately," I offered.

She walked with me back into the trees as the sun set fiery red over the valley.

"We don't have much time," I told her. "So I'm going to make this quick. You've said I can't make you happy."

She bit her lip.

"I will do all that is in my power to honor your wishes," I told her. "We will perform this spell together, and then I will set you free."

"You're going to be part of the spell?" she asked.

She didn't know about the change of plans. Jonah had volunteered to provide the last ingredient needed, but I talked to him about it earlier.

"You need the blood of a shifter. That's going to be me," I told her. "I decided to take Jonah's place. I expect I'll be recovering somewhere until the sun comes up tomorrow. That will keep you safe from me, and we can go our separate ways."

She let out a single sob, and then nodded.

"Cori, if this isn't what you want, all you have to do is say it," I told her. "But at least tell me why."

"You need my magic to make a shifter baby," she said, her voice strained with emotion. "But my magic screws up everything it touches. It's one thing to ruin a statue or a potted plant. But I just can't take that chance on a baby. I'm sorry."

But she turned on her heel, leaving me to chastise myself for making her explain. Rejecting me was hard for her, that much was clear. I hadn't wanted to make it harder.

If I was better at being human, I could help her, make her understand. But I wasn't. I was better off as a bear. Alone.

Before I could do anything else, Anya called for us all to gather, and I sucked in a long breath of cold, sweet air.

I was nothing and nobody. I had lost my mother to my human fears. I was losing my mate to my feral nature. I was a useless, unloved creature with nothing to offer.

Nothing but my shifter blood…

Tonight I would save the others with my blood sacrifice. It was all I had to give, and I would give it gladly to keep them safe.

36

CORI

Anya, Kendall, Nina and Lark marched over to me as I came out of the woods. The four of them looked like an army regiment, swooping in to rescue a fallen soldier.

Broken as my heart was, I felt it warm a little at the sight of my fierce, amazing friends.

"Are you okay?" Kendall demanded.

"I'm f-fine," I told her.

"Good," Anya said. "We need to get started."

The winter ravens on her shoulders squawked and scolded softly, like they were reiterating what she said.

"Did anyone come up with a silver dagger?" I asked.

It hadn't seemed like an impossible item to find compared to the others, but it had been the last one left on the list this morning.

"Sure did," Kendall said, slipping something out of her pocket.

Headmistress Hart's silver letter opener sparkled in the setting sun light.

"Holy cow, you stole it?" I asked as she handed it to me.

"I borrowed it," Kendall said, shrugging. "Hopefully, I can put it back before she notices. We didn't exactly have a lot of fancy silverware around here to choose from."

"You would think an actual castle would have good silver," Nina said thoughtfully. "Aren't people always sitting around polishing it in fairytales?"

"Not if the castle is guarded by shifters," Lark reminded her. "They're not exactly fans of silver."

"Oh," Nina said. "Right."

"Ready?" Anya asked, glancing at the darkening sky.

"Let's do it," Kendall said.

We headed toward the circle together, and I felt a tingle of power in the air. The fellowship of witches was magical, we were told that at school daily, but tonight that thread of strength actually flowed through my sisters into me. It lifted me, in spite of my broken heart, giving me something to hold onto.

When we reached the circle, Anya, Kendall, Nina and Lark each stood at one compass point.

I stayed back. My role was to bleed the guardian, that I now knew would be Reed instead of Jonah.

It was more of an honorary role than a magical one. I hadn't wanted a place in the circle, where my unpredictable magic could threaten the mission, or my friends. None of them had argued with me.

Anya began to read from the scroll that Nina and Lark had written with the beetle ink and raven quill.

The words sounded like some sort of embellished Latin. I didn't understand them, and hadn't even asked Nina and Lark for the translation. The sound was haunting enough when I didn't know.

In the valley below, I could just make out where the

Order's circle had formed. It was lit with a dome of magical energy, a sort of mist lifting and swirling inside it.

The wind on the bluff picked up, lifting Anya's hair as she read, so that she almost looked like she was underwater. There was something strange about her eyes... they were *glowing*. I'd never seen anything like that before.

Nina, Lark and Kendall chanted along with her, repeating the ends of her lines, like a trio of back-up blues singers.

I pulled the small wooden box of ashes from my cloak and plunged the letter opener into it - ceremonially cleaning the silver blade in the ashes of the ancient tree, as the spell required.

I was ready for my part. Well, as ready as I would ever be to stab someone I cared about.

Reed approached me, head down so that I couldn't see his golden eyes. He offered me his forearm and for a moment I stared down at the muscled flesh of the man I loved, wondering how I could even consider marring it.

But the wind was howling now, seeming to grow angrier as the spell progressed, and Anya's chant made the air around the letter opener shiver and blur, as if it had a life of its own.

It was time.

Before I could change my mind, I lifted my hand and brought it down swiftly and cleanly, opening a gash in Reed's arm.

He glanced up at me, as if in shock, and I could see the pain the silver had inflicted on him.

I wished I could take it back. Take all of it back and beg him to claim me.

But it was too late now, his blood was flowing, rich and scarlet, pouring out and soaking into the ground below.

He took a few faltering steps and made it to the circle. The silver must have harmed him even more than I'd imagined it would. Normally, a wound like that would have closed back up in seconds, but the silver was impeding his healing, sapping his strength.

Down in the valley, the mist inside the Order's circle had risen enough to form a sort of storm cloud. It roiled madly, a dark eye in the center.

Our own circle was still dormant, but Anya's eyes glowed pure white now, and her hair swirled straight up over her head. The ravens cried out, their eyes glowing pale blue as if reflecting back a measure of Anya's incredible power.

My quiet friend was normally so diminutive, so gentle. I knew her magic was strong, but I had never pictured her like this. Anya's power seemed to root into the ground below her and lift out into the heavens all around her.

Reed groaned and I was horrified to see the state he was in - barely able to drag himself around the circle. He had nearly made it all the way back to his starting point, he had only a dozen more steps to go.

I moved toward him, hoping I could help him get to the end of the circle.

The air shivered and hummed and the storm from the main spell in the valley below began to be sucked up as if it were in an invisible tunnel, and pulled toward our own counter-spell. The storm writhed and pulsated as it rolled toward us, like a giant slug made of electricity.

I reached Reed, but he pushed me away and staggered forward on his own. Maybe it was important for him to finish on his own.

I stepped back to watch him, wishing with everything in me for him to succeed.

He pushed through the last few paces, and the circle

pulsed with an unearthly glow as he sealed it with his magical blood. He looked ready to collapse, but instead, his head snapped up in alarm.

I followed his sightline and screamed to my friends when I spotted the source of his panic, though the wind and storm swallowed up the sound as it left my lips.

37

REED

With a final, tremendous effort, I dragged my weakened body a few more inches until my blood soaked into the last of the circle.

A flash of power shivered through the air, lighting the circle as my life force sealed the magic.

I was done, and ready to rest, until a terrible scent reached me.

I rose, my whole body stiff with terror.

The masked rider from the gorge was approaching from the hillside below, the wind blowing his hood back just enough for me to catch a glimpse of his bronze hair. An enchanted arrow was already nocked in his bow, ready to kill.

But it was the flaming mane and tail of the vicious stallion that froze my heart. The creature looked even bigger than before somehow. Its hooves pounded the ground furiously as they approached, dark nostrils flaring.

My big body, my anchor of strength, was failing me now. Pain seared my veins and my feet felt like they were made of lead.

But I had to protect the witches. I couldn't let the counter spell fail. And I wouldn't let anything happen to Cori.

With the last of my strength, I staggered into the woods to meet the nightmare and its rider. If I could distract them, even for a few minutes, maybe Anya would have time to finish her spell.

I had to cut them off in the trees before they reached the bluff to keep them out of arrow-range of the circle. The witches couldn't take cover from those magical bolts. They were sitting ducks.

I was their only hope.

38

CORI

Anya was almost disappearing before my eyes, her skin so pale it looked translucent. Her hair swirled over her head and her gown floated around her small form as if caught in an invisible current.

The storm funneling from the circle in the valley into ours pulsed and doubled in on itself. Something strange was happening. Something we hadn't planned for.

The Order of the Broken Blade hadn't been able to let the Raven King through the veil. Our counter spell must have worked. But it seemed like we hadn't merely stopped them at the last minute. We had started something of our own on this side.

And something was happening to Anya.

But I was wrenched out of my fears for my friend in an instant when I heard a howl of pain coming from my mate.

I whirled around to find Reed, hating myself for not going to him when he collapsed from completing the circle. But he wasn't on his hands and knees at the edge of the circle.

He was nowhere to be seen.

I closed my eyes and felt in the darkness for the bond I had rejected.

Reed, where are you?

There was an unmistakable tug on my soul, as if I'd caught my gown on the railing of the great staircase again.

My eyes flew open, and I sprinted into the woods, praying I could make it to him in time.

What could have possibly possessed him to chase after the Order in his condition? I had seen the flaming stallion in his mind the moment I opened the bond. It was terrifying, even to me. Reed was afraid of fire, and had one foot in the grave after his sacrifice.

The branches ripped at my gown, but I didn't care that I was stumbling over roots and brambles, as long as I was moving closer to my mate at top speed.

Magic sizzled in my blood and skittered across my skin, unbidden. Waves of power washed through my chest, sending a delirium of awareness through me.

I could hear the gasping breaths my mate drew in all the way down on the hillside. I could smell the bitter leather of the rider's tack, taste the river on the wind sweeping up from the valley.

My muscles burned from the chase, and when Reed and the rider were finally in view, it was all I could do to stop.

Reed clung to the saddle, too weak to shift, trying to pull the rider down as the horse's fiery mane set his long hair alight.

The trees around them were burning already. The whole forest was about to go up in flames if no one put a stop to it right now.

"Reed," I screamed. But he was fighting for his life with the last of his strength, too focused to hear me.

Together, we might be able to best this single warlock, but I could already see the other riders coming up the hillside to join the first.

It was the perfect time to give in to panic.

But instead, a wave of calm settled over me, cold as ice.

I stood, feet shoulder width apart, palms facing upward, just like I'd been taught.

And called on my powers.

Not a hint of magic. Not just enough to power a spell. Not holding back to try to keep from messing things up.

I called it all.

There was no time to meditate, and no amount of meditation that could pay in advance for the magic I needed. This was no parlor trick or school assignment. I was going to wipe them out.

I inhaled the night air and exhaled into my right hand.

A tiny storm cloud formed about my palm.

Time to grow, Misty, I told it in my mind. *Time to finally show them what we can do.*

She didn't bite me this time, didn't resist. Instead she expanded - to the size of cotton candy at the town fair, the size of a globe, a hot air balloon.

Power blossomed inside me, but I felt no fear. For the first time in my life, I wasn't afraid of my magic. I *wanted* to do harm. I would blast this mountaintop from its base to punish the ones who would harm my mate.

My storm cloud rose and unfurled toward the riders.

I screamed, letting the emotion flow from me like pure energy.

Fingers of lighting blasted from the cloud, charring the grass.

One of the horses reared up and bucked its rider, who

fell to the ground and nicked himself with his own enchanted arrow.

There was a small explosion that killed the rider instantly and spooked two more of those horrible horses.

Their riders cried out in fear and pain, and then I heard another howl of muted agony and remembered that the forest was burning around my mate.

Release, I told my storm. *Let it go.*

There was a moment when the Earth seemed to go still.

Then the air pressure changed so suddenly my ears clicked, and the rain began to fall.

The first fat drops hissed against the horse's tails and ran down my cheeks like tears. Then it lashed down in sheets, extinguishing all the fire.

The trees were still smoldering but the danger of losing the whole forest had passed.

Reed's moans ceased, and the horses whinnied piteously. They looked small and strange without their dancing manes of fire.

The power was blazing from me now and the rain came down in buckets, lightning flashing so that that whole hillside strobed.

One of the riders ran at me, arrow cocked and ready.

I lifted one hand and a lightning bolt felled him.

But another had been flanking me.

Suddenly Reed was flying at him, shifting in midair to tackle him to the ground.

As they fell, I spotted two more men and one of the nightmares behind them. The horse snorted and its fiery mane flared to life once more. It reared up to pummel Reed while he was down.

"No," I screamed, instinctively pressing my palms through the air.

A brand-new thunder storm was birthed from each of my hands and launched forward toward the monstrous horse.

I felt the power tearing from me, emptying me, but I couldn't stop. I wouldn't stop until he was safe, until every last creature that stood against us was obliterated.

My chest ached and my vision tinged with red. In the back of my mind, I knew what was happening, but I didn't care.

Rain was flying straight out of my fingers now, not even waiting for new clouds to be formed. I ejected lightning out of my fingertips, and it felt like it was being ripped from my skull. I let the magic tear the power from my insides, and the sky flashed purple with it.

But I had let the emotion get the best of me.

While I went off like a firework, Reed was still trying to fight off the last horse. It had gotten the better of him and he had shifted back to human again, unable to sustain the bear form in his weakened state.

He screamed and I turned to him, lifting up my palms to send a burst of energy to protect him.

But there was nothing left in me.

Professor Sora had described the end point of used up magic as a wall, but this was so much more. It was a barrier made of glass, invisible and unending. I pressed my consciousness against the cool, unfeelingness of it, desperate for a charge.

And when I found nothing, I let my eyes rest on my mate's desperate, golden ones. I could feel him slipping away from me. The knowledge of him, of us, sliding from my mind like the water flowing away all around us.

If I didn't stop pushing, I would lose the memory of him

forever. If I pushed too far, I could lose it all, memories of my magic, my friends... myself.

"No, Cori," he moaned.

I closed my eyes and shattered my wall.

39

CORI

It wasn't raining, but the air smelled like ozone.

I blinked up at the starry sky and into the startlingly golden eyes of a beautiful man whose expression wavered between relief and sorrow.

His hair was ragged, and parts of it looked burned. There was ash on his dirty face, but clean streaks striped it. He must have been crying.

"Where am I?" I asked him.

But he opened his mouth only to close it again without answering.

"Cori," a woman's voice said softly.

I turned my head and saw that several more people knelt by my side. The one closest to me had birds on her shoulders. They looked like crows but with all the color drained out of them.

Cori. That sounds familiar...

"Cori, you probably don't remember much," said a woman with purple cat-eye glasses. "You just had a very traumatic experience."

Cori was me? Now we were getting somewhere.

"Cori," I said softly, trying it out.

It was a nice name, plaintive and neutral. I tried to picture what kind of a person might be called by that name, but I got nowhere with that, so I looked down at my body instead.

I was draped in a gown, just like the women who were looking at me.

"What... happened?" I asked.

"You're a very powerful witch," the woman with the glasses replied. "You stopped a forest fire, and you saved someone's life."

"I did?" I asked.

I didn't know who I was. Was I the sort of person who normally accomplished acts of heroism?

"You did," she said.

"That doesn't feel right," I told her honestly. "It doesn't feel like me."

"You did it for love," the sad man said. "You did it to save me."

"I love you?" I asked him.

He certainly looked lovable, with those beautiful eyes and that sad smile. I kind of liked the idea of loving him.

But my question upset him, and he turned away from me, sobbing silently.

"It's not her fault," a woman with a long blonde ponytail snapped at the sad man. "Her price is memory loss. She did this to save your ass."

"Kendall," the little one with the birds scolded.

"Why should I mince words?" the one called Kendall demanded. "Who would that help? Why should he expect anything different from her? She did this for *him*. She paid the ultimate price for *him,* and all he can do is cry?"

"Cori, I'm so sorry," he moaned, turning back to me.

"I'm okay," I told him.

It felt weird to have him so sad, and everyone yelling, when I didn't even know what was going on.

But he was so handsome, and I was curious. What an amazing life I must have had, if this man was the one I loved - the one who loved me enough to be broken by my confusion.

"Are you hungry?" he asked.

"Yes," I said, without having to think about it.

"Can I take you home?" he asked.

"Sure," I said. "Where do I live?"

He looked helplessly at the others, but they seemed to be at a loss.

When he turned back to me, his expression was determined.

"Once upon a time," he said, lifting me in his arms, "there was a woman with powers beyond imagining."

I nuzzled his broad, warm chest and the scent of him was familiar.

"She lived in an enormous castle," he went on. "And everyone who knew her loved her, because she was kind and funny, and even humble in spite of her incredible magic."

A castle. He was telling me I lived in a castle.

"Am I... a princess?" I asked dubiously.

"You're a witch," he said.

Something whispered beneath my skin, a faint tickle and hum of magic.

Yes, yes, that's right...

A massive castle had appeared as we walked. It loomed over us, dark and forbidding, but somehow the sight of it filled me with relief.

"That's Primrose Academy," he whispered. "It's your school, and your home, and it's my home too."

"You're a witch?" I asked.

He chuckled and a wave of pleasure went through me, as if his delight played out through my neurons.

"I'm a shifter," he told me. "A bear. It's my job to live in the tower and protect the school."

"And to love me," I remembered.

"Yes, and to love you." He glanced down at me, and I saw hope as well as sadness in those golden eyes.

"Why are you sad?" I asked as he pushed open the doors to the castle.

"You were meant to be my mate," he told me. "It's complicated. But we had to spend three nights together, and then you would decide if you wanted us to be bound together forever. Tonight will be the fourth night. Our time to decide is about to be over."

Wow. He was right. That was complicated.

"Now what happens?" I asked.

"I'm not sure," he admitted. "But I don't think a full mate bond will be possible if we let another night pass."

Tears were hot in my eyes and I buried my face in the crook of his neck. It was as if my body remembered what my brain could not.

I felt his pang of sympathy as if it were my own.

"Oh," I said, pulling back.

"What's wrong?" he asked.

"I think I can... feel your emotions," I said. "Is that possible?"

"That's part of a mate bond," he said, nodding.

"Will we lose that?" I asked.

His jaw clenched and he nodded.

"I don't want to lose it," I said without thinking.

"Cori, what are you saying?" he stopped in the middle of the dark hallway, fixing me with his golden eyes.

"I'm saying I want us to seal the bond," I decided.

"But you don't even know me," he protested. "You don't even know you."

"Is this something I wanted before?" I asked.

He paused before answering.

"You did want it," he told me carefully. "You wanted it badly, I think. But you were afraid that your control over magic wasn't good enough for you to be a mother to shifter children."

"Was I right?" I asked.

He shook his head.

"You should have seen yourself tonight. You were like a god."

For an instant I *could* see it as he saw it, his memory of me standing tall and proud, lightning shooting out of my fingers like some kind of comic book superhero.

"I can see it when you think about it," I said. "Just a little. I don't remember it, but I can see it."

He smiled encouragingly and I was almost breathless at the beauty of that smile. I could sense that it was rare, and tender, and meant only for me.

"I want to seal our bond," I told him again. "I don't really know what's going on. And I don't really care. But I do know that I never want to lose this feeling."

"Cori," he groaned. "Please don't tempt me. I want that more than anything, but it's not right. If you don't remember, you can't choose."

"Will I ever remember?" I asked.

"No," he said simply, clearly struggling to hold his emotions in check. "Your friend was right. You used so much magic that the price you paid is permanent. You will never remember."

I let the idea of it hit me fully, breathing it in and out until it was familiar.

I was going to have to relearn my entire life.

And I suspected that the best thing in it was about to be lost to me, unless I could change his mind in the next few hours.

"I understand," I said.

"I'm sorry, Cori," he told me.

"I'm not," I decided. "If I did it to save you, then it was worth it."

He pressed his lips to the crown of my head and the sensation sent thrills through me.

"If I did it to save you, then I obviously wanted to be your mate," I told him.

"Yes," he said. "But I can't claim you when you're still in confusion."

"There's nothing confusing about this," I said, the anger rising in me. "The man I love is telling me that a woman I don't remember is going to stop us from being together. Right?"

"I... I don't know," he admitted.

"No," I said firmly. "She's not going to do that. *I'm* going to choose."

I pressed my lips to his cheek, his chin, his neck. Each kiss felt like home. My body was coming to life in his arms.

"I choose you," I told him. "I want you."

Then he was running, blasting a door half off its hinges, and running up what felt like an endless flight of stairs.

40

REED

My heart and body were thundering with need, but my mind was still torn to bits.

How could I claim her when she couldn't remember?

What if she never forgave me?

Cori's cruel little mouth was still pressing kisses to my neck and I held back a roar of frustration.

She seemed...different than before. She was more confident, less timid. I liked this version of my mate. I loved the easy confidence, even if I couldn't understand where it was coming from.

Shouldn't she be frightened?

We reached the top of the stairs at last, and I stepped into my room, placed her gently back on her feet, and locked the door behind us.

By the time I turned around, she was already stepping out of her gown, that sweet, curvy body bared for me.

"Cori," I moaned.

"Have we done this before?" she asked placing her open palms on my chest and closing her eyes.

Her question called up memories of what she had felt like, writhing and moaning under my hands in the bathtub that second night.

"OH," she sighed. "What did we do on the third night?"

"It's complicated," I told her, remembering the hike through the woods and the baby birds.

"You can explain about the birds and the hike another night," she decided. "We don't have much time."

I glanced at the windows. Dawn was coming. The night had faded from velvet black to blue. If we let this night pass, we might lose our chance to seal the bond.

"Are you sure about this?" I asked her, as my body strained toward hers.

"Yes, but I'm starting to think you aren't," she said. "Did you have reservations before?"

"None," I lied.

My reservations had always been about *me*, not about her.

And it seemed like hers had been the same.

"Then *hurry*," she demanded.

We were two of a kind. And I was tired of denying it. I began tearing off my own clothes.

If we were going to start over creating new memories together, I was determined to make this first one count.

41

CORI

I crawled into his bed, trying not to get hung up on the fact that I didn't even know his name. I was pretty sure if I admitted that much, I'd have to start over again convincing him to claim me.

And we were so deliciously close.

I could sense his hesitation, and I couldn't blame him - the situation was... unique, and he didn't want to take advantage. He needed to be sure it was what I really wanted. But I had never been more sure of anything in my life.

He crawled in after me, pinning me to the bed with the weight of his muscular form.

His first kiss was gentle, his second hot as lightning.

I kissed him back, every cell in me filling with joy at his touch.

He pulled away from my mouth to kiss my cheeks, my eyelids, the place where my neck met my shoulder.

I arched my back, and he ravaged my breasts while I howled with pleasure.

When he abandoned my chest to nuzzle my belly, I tangled my hands in his hair, urging him lower.

He let out a growl and buried himself between my thighs.

The sensation of his tongue against my sex was so sweet it was almost painful. I moaned and lifted my hips for more.

But he crawled back up to me, caging my head between his arms.

"It's time," he whispered, glancing up at the window.

Dawn was coming.

"Yes," I told him, wrapping my legs around his hips.

"Cori," he said pleadingly. His jaw was tense with restrained need. I appreciated what it took for him to do what he thought was right and offer me one last out.

"My past is gone," I told him. "All I can see is a future ahead of me with you. And I want it so much."

His golden eyes were so beautiful, wet with tears and luminous with emotion.

He guided himself against me and I felt a pinching pain and then a wave of exquisite pleasure as he sank inside me.

"God, Cori," he groaned.

I couldn't answer, I was experiencing the claiming twice, once through my senses and again through his. I could feel him deep inside me and myself sheathing him, all our pleasure and emotion - I was drowning in it and I wanted more, more, more.

He withdrew and plunged in again, roaring out his pleasure.

I cried out, clinging to him, tilting my hips up for more.

He gave me what I wanted until the pleasure had me shaking and straining for release.

"Mine," he growled at last, nuzzling my neck and biting down.

There was muted pain but there was far more pleasure. I

felt a touch of my blood touch his tongue and the bond tighten and lock around us.

He swirled his tongue against my tender flesh as if in apology and it was too much for me.

"Please," I whimpered.

Expertly, he slid a big hand between our bodies and massaged my throbbing little pearl.

The pleasure lifted me up and for a moment I was flying.

I could hear his hoarse cries as his own pleasure took him over the edge.

We clung to each other until the waves of ecstasy let us go at last and we fell back on the bed, panting as the first rays of dawn slipped in the windows of the tower.

42

CORI

I sat at the diner in the little town at the bottom of the mountain from Primrose Academy, Reed's arm slung around my shoulder.

We had been out of the tower only twice in the last couple of days - both times to get food.

We spent most of our time in bed, getting to know each other, starting my new life with a foundation of love.

Through his eyes, I had seen so much of our time together. I knew so much more now about the girl I had once been.

But I liked the woman I was now much better.

"What are you thinking about?" he asked, his rough thumb stroking the upward curve of my lip.

"I'm happy," I told him honestly.

"Hey, lovebirds," Kendall said, sliding into the booth beside me.

"Hi Kendall," I said.

She reached for one of my fries and I smacked her hand.

"Nope, I'm hungry," I told her. "Get your own."

She gave me a funny look and then shook her head.

"What?" I asked.

"You're different now, that's all," she said with a wry grin.

"Would the old me have wanted to share her fries with you?" I asked.

"No," Kendall said. "Definitely not. But she wouldn't have stopped me."

"Hey guys," Bella called out as she and Luke approached. "Nina, Lark and Anya are on their way in too."

"Hi," I said.

Luke and Reed exchanged nods and the others filed in.

The waitress had been surprised when I asked her to pull a big table up to our booth, but we definitely needed it.

"So... how's it going, Cori?" Bella asked, when everyone had settled in.

"Fine," I told her. "I still don't remember anything, if that's what you're asking. But I can see a bit through Reed's eyes. Enough to know what we all mean to each other. I'm looking forward to getting to know everyone. Again."

"Yeah," she said, smiling. "I guess that's pretty good."

"It *is* pretty good," I said, squeezing Reed's hand under the table. "But I think we all really want to know what happened in the valley, with the other circle."

"Sure," she said. "It was pretty intense."

"They started off just like you guys," Luke explained. "They cleared a circle while we watched from the trees."

"Whose blood did they use?" Reed asked. There was an edge to his voice I didn't like. I wondered if there was something the old me would have known.

"They poured it from a chalice," Luke said, shaking his head.

Reed nodded once, his jaw tight.

"When they read their spell, the smoke that lifted from the circle was starting to take the shape of a man, the Raven

King," Bella said. "It wasn't until your spell got underway that the smoke was dragged out of shape. Did you do that, Cori?"

"That was Anya," Kendall said. "She went so bright she almost disappeared. She was like some kind of supernova. What *was* that, Anya?"

"No idea," Anya said, looking uncomfortable. "Whatever it was, I'm just glad it worked."

"The Order came too close," Bella said. "We're really lucky Cori did what she did to shut them down."

"But that won't be the last of them," Luke added. "They're furious at our interference, and more determined than ever."

"I can handle them," I said. "I'm not afraid anymore."

It was true, I had seen the fear in that other Cori's eyes. It wouldn't exist in mine. Smashing through that barrier in my magic had *opened* me. I had access to my full power now, and control over it. I didn't need to be afraid anymore.

In time, my new life would merge with the old Cori's, as I settled into the warmth of her friendships and the adventures of her days.

But this core of confidence wasn't going anywhere. It was going to be the strong foundation that I needed to move forward.

"*We* can handle them," Reed said, leaning over to press his lips to my hair. "We'll have each other's backs, no matter what."

"Uh... are you guys ready?" the waitress asked, staring agog at Kendall.

I glanced over at my friend to see that she had a couple of drops of water clinging together in a ball, hovering over her glass as she moved her hand back and forth gently, playing with them.

Bella cleared her throat and the water dropped back in the cup as Kendall looked up.

"Yes, we're very ready," I told the waitress with a smile. "We're as ready as we can be."

And looking around at my friends and my mate, I knew it was true. Whatever was going to happen next, we were ready to face it.

Together.

Thanks for reading Bear Charm!

Are you ready to find out what kind of trouble Kendall gets into when she makes contact with the shifter brother Luke and Reed have been searching for all this time? And are you dying to know exactly who her secret boyfriend is, and what he thinks about this whole mess?

Then make sure you order your copy of Panther Curse right away!

Panther Curse
https://www.tashablack.com/shiftersbewitched.html

TASHA BLACK STARTER LIBRARY

Packed with steamy shifters, mischievous magic, billionaire superheroes, and plenty of HEAT, the Tasha Black Starter Library is the perfect way to dive into Tasha's unique brand of Romance with Bite!
Get your FREE books now at tashablack.com!

ABOUT THE AUTHOR

Tasha Black lives in a big old Victorian in a tiny college town. She loves reading anything she can get her hands on, writing paranormal romance, and sipping pumpkin spice lattes.

Get all the latest info, and claim your FREE Tasha Black Starter Library at www.TashaBlack.com

Plus you'll get the chance for sneak peeks of upcoming titles and other cool stuff!

Keep in touch...
www.tashablack.com
authortashablack@gmail.com

facebook.com/romancewithbite
twitter.com/romancewithbite

Printed in Great Britain
by Amazon